Home for the Holidays

A Potter Lake Small Town Romance

Potter Lake
Book 3.5

DL White

BOOKS

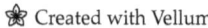

Contents

Home for the Holidays

Author's note

I promise I'm fine, but a Backstreet Boys song just dropped into my head.

"Oh my God, she's back again..."

I hope that this note has found all of my seasoned and new-to-me readers well... and if it hasn't, may this festive and steamy novella lift your spirits. This release is lucky #13 and I've never been so happy to bring something to your faces. I have loved bringing Reid and Sabrina to life in these pages.

A note on this one- there will be an epilogue, but I need more time to do it justice. It will be a freebie, downloadable to your phones and e-readers via book funnel. Be the first to know when it drops by signing up for my newsletter.

I *love* to hear how much people are enjoying my books. Please send any "SHE SAID WHAT?!" to me on any social media site or to my <u>email: authordl at booksbydlwhite dot com</u>. Post any criticism in an honest, balanced review at your fave retail or review site.

I appreciate your time and good opinion and hope you adore this novel.

xoxo,
DL White

Welcome back to Potter Lake

"I need to be clear that I like this. I need this, especially on a day like today, but..."

"That's all it is, Satisfying a need."

Reid Gallagher hasn't returned to Potter Lake because he misses his family, or because he wonders how his hometown has fared since he left. After many years away, this visit is strictly business....until he meets Sabrina.

Sabrina Ward's crumbling marriage drives her to the peace and solace of her Aunt Cara's comfortable home in a slow, southern town. Her stay was always going to be temporary, but for Reid, she might consider an extended stay.

As the first snow blankets Potter Lake in a winter wonderland, Sabrina and Reid give in to an inconvenient yet irresistible spark of attraction. With Reid's departure looming, a lucrative opportunity could turn a casual holiday fling into a chance at love.

Come for the festive holiday vibes... stay for a steamy love story and the charm of Potter Lake, where second chances aren't just possible; they're inevitable. Home for the Holidays is a heartwarming novella, perfect for fans of seasonal Hallmark movies and the magic of the season.

Content Warnings: Divorce, adult language and sexual content including depictions of sex acts on the page. If any of these are a stop sign for you, I encourage you to engage in self care and choose another title.

Chapter One

Reid

THE LOW HUM of tires on pavement hung in the background as I navigated the winding roads from Healy, Georgia to my hometown of Potter Lake. The shadows of the tall pines that lined the road danced before me. The scent of pine needles wafted through the vents, reminding me of riding bikes with my friends on these same streets. My grip on the steering wheel had become tighter over the course of my conversation with Mitchell, my partner at Sterling & Gallagher Development.

"If we don't do it, someone else will."

Mitchell Sterling's throaty voice boomed through the speakers in the car, reminding me that this wasn't purely a social trip. I hadn't returned to Potter Lake because I missed my family, or because I wondered how the small, slow Southern town had fared since I left it after graduating from Healy University. I'd returned because if I didn't complete the land survey, my partner would swoop in and, without a shred of reverence for the idyllic lakeside community, propose an unwelcome footprint of box stores and fast-food restaurants.

From what I'd heard about recent goings-on in Potter Lake, that wouldn't go well. My parents were officially in their golden years, so under the guise of checking in on my family home, I agreed to take some time between Thanksgiving and Christmas to do a cursory check of the town and report back.

"I don't see how you're not excited about this, Reid. It's practically a blank canvas, from what I hear. They're growing at an incredible rate, and there's no doubt they need someone to step in and offer some direction and opportunity, maybe a few modern conveniences."

"Well, it's not Mayberry, Mitch," I replied, knowing Mitchell wasn't really listening for my input but to hear himself speak.

This was our dance. He was a bundle of energy, bursting with enthusiasm and full of ideas. I was slower, methodical. I saw each project as a puzzle and, in my mind, worked out every detail before I even put pen to page. This deal, if it even had a chance to go through, would take finesse.

Mitchell did not have finesse.

"Look, man," I said after letting him ramble for a few minutes. "I'm going to do the job, but respect what I have to say when the survey is over. It might look like a slam dunk on paper, but I'm telling you, there is a reason this town has been slow to develop."

"I'll let you cook, but on a serious tip, you've got until the top of the year before I start moving. I'm not missing out on an opportunity because you're sentimental."

"Man, don't threaten me. Every project needs two affirmative votes before money moves, and you've blocked me on projects before. You need my yes on this, so let me work it out. You will not be able to run these folks over. They'll chase you out with pitchforks."

The sound of Mitchell's laughter bounced around the interior of the spacious Ford Expedition. "Aight, keep me in the loop. I've gotta run, late for a quick nine holes with Zuck."

I rolled my eyes as the call disconnected. Sterling did not know Mark Zuckerberg. One of his best friends was hard at work developing a social network to take on Meta. Mitchell called him Zuck to get under his skin.

I followed the off-ramp from the highway, savoring this drive since it took me along the lake where the surface of the water was smooth as a pane of glass. The potential for new business was always exciting, and Mitchell was right; establishing a presence like a few large convenience stores could be the boost a small town needed to bring in merchandise and services not found anywhere else. The project could also create jobs and bring in revenue. However, there would be opposition to such a venture competing with the existing mom and pop stores.

For example, *my* mom and pop's store. Our family had run Pinkney's Grocery since the town's inception. My maternal grandfather, Ellison Pinkney, first opened the grocery as a roadside stand. The store had been a reliable place to pick up sundries, grain, meat, and fruit my whole life.

Anxiety surged at the thought of mentioning a land survey to my mother.

I turned up the radio, fiddling with the dial to get the local station in clearer. *News and weather on the 5's,* boasted Clyde Fuller, who had been saying the same thing over the air for as long as I could remember. The Temptations' "Let It Snow" floated through the speakers, I let the music settle my nerves as I rolled through the outskirts of town. A pang of nostalgia hit as I passed Bread & Butter Bakery, where I spent afternoons as a kid begging for cinnamon roll scraps.

I steered the vehicle into the driveway of my childhood home and climbed out, filling my lungs with a deep inhale of crisp fall air and freshly cut grass. For a moment, I put aside ulterior motives. I was home.

The screen door swung open with a squeak. My mother's plump, diminutive form stepped out of the house and onto the painted stone porch.

"Well, look who made it!" she called, fists planted on her hips and her lips spread into a wide smile. "You could have called somebody to tell us you were on the way."

"Hey, Mama." We spoke weekly, but her voice in my ears was nothing compared to hearing and seeing her in person. "I almost missed my flight. Then the rental place only had this boat available."

"Don't *hey, Mama* me. Bring your behind up here. I've got dinner on."

I laughed as I climbed the porch steps to my mother's open arms. "You know I'm all about some dinner from your stove."

She hugged me tight, wrapping both arms around me, then pulled back. "Don't seem like you're all about some dinner, son," she said, squeezing my arms. "Are you doing alright? Don't you have somebody to cook up something for you now and again?"

I groaned aloud, reaching behind her for the latch to the screen door. "I'm fit for an almost fifty-year-old man. And that's a clever way to ask if I'm dating. I'm not, by the way."

"I'm not being clever about a thing." She stepped over the threshold to lead the way into a well-furnished home that smelled of everything good in life. "I was happy when you divorced that gal, what's-her-name…"

"Elodie," I supplied. She knew my ex-wife's name enough to talk mess about her during my divorce.

"I know that woman's name," she snapped, heading through the living room to the kitchen, turning on lamps as she went. "And I don't miss her. Had her nose in the air whenever we came to town, like she was doing us a favor by breathing the same air as us."

Mama let out a loud, offended huff while standing at the stove, sliding oven mitts on her hands. "Anyway, if I wanted to know if you had replaced her saddity behind, I would have asked. I don't have to be clever about a thing."

"Okay, Mama," I replied, staving off a long lecture. "Renita and Rachel sent me photos from Thanksgiving. Looks like it was a nice spread."

"You just missed them." She opened the oven door and reared back for a few moments to let the steam escape, then reached in to pull out several covered dishes. "They brought the husbands and kids and everything. How was the holiday with your son and...*her*?"

"It was an okay time. You know Elodie likes a party. She had a house full of people and a big catered dinner."

"*Hmph.* It would have been nice if she let you bring Joshua to Thanksgiving instead of making you go all the way to Atlanta for a big dinner full of people that aren't his family. She don't like him being out of her sight and I don't like that. And who ever heard of a catered Thanksgiving?"

"Her family *is* his family. And I know Pinkney's has been selling fully cooked dinners for years."

"That's different than having some restaurant cook up your holiday meal. Ain't no love in those mashed potatoes."

My mama was not wrong about that, and I wouldn't dare argue if she was. Instead, I reached for a roll from the pan she brought out of the oven. She smacked my hand, but not fast enough. I pulled the roll apart to watch the steam rise and the butter bubble, then popped half of it into my mouth.

"Mmmmm! Nothing but love in this roll."

"Already picking at the food. Get on out of here! Go find your father. He's out in the garden. I'm sure he wants to say hello."

I pulled off my jacket and slipped my tie from around my

neck. A few days of being up under my mother and not wearing a suit and silk tie for ten hours a day was just what I needed. I hung both from a chair and walked through the kitchen and mudroom to the back door.

The acreage behind the house was a lush carpet of green grass, then a vegetable garden plot bordered by thick woods that stretched out to the property line. I spotted the outline of my father with his back to me, leaning over and tending to the dirt. I trampled through his grass in my Italian leather shoes but didn't care. As I got closer, I saw he was pulling carrots from the ground and tossing them into a basket.

"Hey, old man," I said as I reached him, my feet crunching fallen leaves.

He slowly straightened, squinting at me, then breaking into a grin. "Well, look who it is!" he called, his voice cracking.

I grabbed him up in a gentle bear hug. He was thin but sturdy, well-muscled from years of working in the garden and stocking shelves at the store.

"I was wonderin' when you would come through," he said, pulling back from the hug with a clap on the shoulder. "I ain't heard you pull up. Been out here trying to get the last of the harvest. The temperature is supposed to drop low soon."

He went back to work, asking over his shoulder, "Your mama seen you?"

"She's about to serve dinner. She sent me out here to get you because I was getting on her nerves."

"You know how she is about her kitchen. Why you think I'm out here?" His laugh came out in a wheeze. Cliff Gallagher was not a man who liked to sit around doing nothing, but at his age, exerting himself in the sun could not be the best thing.

"Tell you what, Dad. You come on in, have some dinner. I'll help you finish up out here tomorrow. We should have time to get everything in before the temperature drops, right?"

"Now that's a deal," he said, offering a hand for me to shake. He held on tight for me to pull him from the clump of dirt. I threw an arm over his shoulder and walked with him back to the house.

Over a sumptuous feast, the conversation flowed easily—stories of my life in a suburb on the outskirts of Cleveland, Mama's updates on the neighbors and their various antics, developments at Pinkney's and the businesses around Potter Lake. These days, they left the store in the capable hands of their management staff, but they still dropped by most days to get in the way and gossip with residents.

Despite my best efforts to keep things light and focused on our personal lives, I couldn't ignore a nagging urge to broach the reason for my visit.

"Hey, Mama," I said hesitantly, testing the waters. "Remember when Mayor Adams was selling off land around here? And offering space for folks to open businesses?"

"When he was trying to kill this town, you mean?" Her whole face bunched up with her scowl. She may as well have cursed. "Thank goodness for Mayor Cavanaugh. And Leslie, too. You remember her?"

I nodded. Leslie was much younger than me, having just entered high school when I left Potter Lake. I'd heard the stories about her returning to the town to run the beauty shop and feuding with the owner of one of the new shops on the other side of the lake. He ran against Mayor Adams, unseating him after a long tenure in office, and married Leslie. Together, they were bringing so much change to the city.

It was encouraging to me. Maybe I could get them to see my proposal as a good thing.

Mama's thick, gray brows furrowed as she quizzically

stared from across the table. "Why are you asking about Quincy?"

"Uhm... I'm not," I stammered. "I mean, not really asking about him. I was asking about the land. If you knew of any still up for grabs around here."

"Reid Gallagher," she warned, her eyes narrowing suspiciously. "Don't go thinking we are so old that we don't remember what you do for a living. Potter Lake is not in need of any big changes like those developments you build. We're growing slow but doing fine as we are."

"Of course," I agreed, sucking down a mouthful of sweet lemonade to help swallow the lump in my throat. "I was just asking, Mama."

"And I've answered. Let's leave business talk for another day. You still like pound cake with strawberries, don't you?"

"Yes, ma'am, I do," I replied, offering her a weak smile.

Chapter Two

Sabrina

"I CANNOT WATCH this one more time," I murmured to myself, snapping off the TV on the way to the kitchen table.

Of course, the only Atlanta station that came in clearly in Potter Lake would be doing a story on my husband Adrian. The fistfight he'd been involved in with his mistresses' husband was the biggest, juiciest scoop any newsroom had seen a while.

I took a seat across from my Aunt Cara, who reminded me of Olympia Dukakis. Sweet, Southern, silver-haired...and spicy. She loved a good bit of gossip, so much that I questioned my decision to hole up at her house while this controversy with Adrian blew over.

"This too shall pass." Aunt Cara poured us both a glass of wine and set the bottle on the table between us. "How are you holding up, honey?"

"I feel like I'm suffocating," I replied, stabbing my fork into my plate.

My face flushed at the recollection of that fight. It was on YouTube for the world to see and be repeated, ad nauseam, until the end of time. Or at least the two-week news cycle. I prayed for something of worldwide importance to happen so the incident would be wiped off every broadcast.

"Not only is my marriage over, but the whole world—or at least the state—became witness to it falling apart. They can watch it, frame by frame, over and over and over."

"Well, now…" Aunt Cara began around a mouthful of chicken, vegetables, and flaky crust. "I thought you planned to leave him."

"At the end of the year! Not…*now*. Not this way." I pinched the bridge of my nose to hold the tears at bay. I'd cried enough. "I wanted to leave with dignity and grace, not with my dirty laundry aired out for all to see."

"You wanted to have the upper hand."

"That, too."

"Po-tay-to, po-tah-to," Aunt Cara replied. "I don't understand the reaction if you planned to leave anyway."

"Because it's ending with me looking like I didn't know he was cheating, like I didn't know he spends three hours every Wednesday at a downtown Atlanta hotel. I'm not mad he was cheating, I'm mad he got caught up in some brawl with that woman's husband at the fucking Regency."

I gulped wine, trying but failing to steel my emotions.

"And what about my career? I'm a laughingstock."

As a Senior Asset Manager at Aegis Financial, Adrian was not my direct supervisor, but it was assumed among most associates that I'd slept my way to middle management. I'd worked my ass off to land a role where my talents had an opportunity to shine. I was great at my job and never let being married to someone on the executive floor affect the passion that infused my work. My team and I were close, and having this drama unfold with everyone watching was an actual nightmare.

"My director couldn't wait to approve my request for a leave of absence. I bet I never get another job in finance."

"Sabrina, that's nonsense," Aunt Cara said, pointing with her fork before going in for another serving. "You are allowed to be hurt, to be upset, but you don't have to live there. Have some dinner. Your mother's chicken pot pie recipe will make those maudlin thoughts disappear."

A wistful smile made my lips turn up. Cooking my mother's recipes was the best way to remember her. She passed away when I was young, leaving me in the care of her favorite sister, my Aunt Cara. She and my uncle had been the best surrogate parents I could have ever asked for.

Too bad none of us saw Adrian for who he really was before I walked down the aisle in a designer gown and an explosion of pink roses.

"Besides, you weren't fired. Your director said to take some time away, and it was good advice to do so. And you know what the young ladies say—the best way to get over a man is to get under a new one."

"Aunt Cara, I am still married!"

"Barely," she conceded, "and only technically, but you planned to leave at the end of this year, and Adrian is obviously done. You're here in a town where you have no roots, and no one knows who you are except for me. The stage is set."

Aunt Cara shot a sly smile across the table, her eyes twinkling with mischief. "Maybe you'll meet someone who offers a bit of...*distraction*."

Her brow lifted and lowered as she paused to sip her wine.

"Here?" I scoffed, spooning up another bite. "I came here because this town is full of people who probably don't know who Adrian is, and if they do, don't care. Although, seeing as how my aunt knows everyone's business, that might have been a mistake."

I was still reeling from the stories she had shared since I arrived a few days ago. None of this town's secrets were safe.

Their tales of unrequited love and lifelong grudges had been spilled over glasses of wine and slices of pound cake. I wasn't sure I wanted to meet any of the people Cara described, but she insisted they were mostly harmless.

"It wouldn't hurt to meet some people. Were you planning to hide out in the house for months on end?"

"I hadn't really got that far in planning, but it sounds like a good idea to me. What do you do all day since you retired and moved out here?"

While I finished a healthy portion of chicken pot pie, Aunt Cara plied me with stories about how she spent her days in Potter Lake. Between her garden club, the Silver Sneakers Walking Group, her book club, the auxiliary volunteer group, and especially her bi-weekly appointment at the Curl & Dye, her calendar stayed full. She and her friend Angela, whose husband served on city council, always scheduled their appointments together so they could get in their time to catch up on other people's business.

I listened with half an ear, my mind still on our earlier conversation about Adrian. And...well, moving on from Adrian. The idea of rebound sex was not an unattractive one.

Adrian and I had run hot and cold for the last few years. I had noticed that his attentions had shifted to younger and more...*petite* women. I'd caught Adrian's eye when I was younger and thinner. I was secure enough in my marriage to relax, but I wasn't displeased with the womanly, shapely figure I had developed.

He'd made it clear that despite always dressing to impress, I could drop some weight, but not to bother because I was too old and tired to turn heads.

If I'd been smart, I would have also been cheating. I'd spent so much time setting myself up to walk out of his life that I hadn't thought to retaliate with someone who appreciated a woman with something to hang onto.

Aunt Cara and I finished our meals and wine. While she

retired to the living room, I picked up her plate and headed to the sink, rinsed the dishes and silverware, and placed them in the dishwasher. Unlike our penthouse condo, her kitchen had a large picture window that looked over the property behind her house. It was so country and cheerful.

As I finished sweeping the kitchen floor, I glanced out of the window to admire the sunset. I was surprised to see two men in the yard next door, one older, one younger. I assumed the older man was Cliff Gallagher. Aunt Cara had mentioned she and the Gallaghers were the same age.

"Aunt Cara, do the neighbors have children?"

"They sure do. Their daughters were just here. Why? What are you looking at?"

Cara appeared next to me, craning her neck to see what had caught my attention. Her eyes narrowed for a moment before she shook her head. "Now, I'd remember that fine young man. Patricia has been beside herself because her son was coming to visit. He hasn't been back to Potter Lake in years. Must be him."

"Interesting," I mumbled, watching as the man disappeared inside the Gallagher home.

"Isn't it, though?" Cara replied with a knowing smile. "Potter Lake is small, but never boring."

Aunt Cara suggested a walk around the block before we turned in for the night. She pulled a light sweater over her blouse and slipped her feet into a pair of sneakers with a bright pink swoosh along the side. "My step counter says I'm short for the day, and I'm in a competition. Earline won't beat me this month."

I grabbed a hoodie and pulled it on over my t-shirt, catching myself in the mirror to be sure it settled on my hips, and followed her out the door. As we walked, Cara chatted about the houses we passed, who lived where, and what their history was. She had only lived in Potter Lake for a few years, but the way people stepped out to wave, to say hello, to exchange stories, you'd have thought she had been born and raised in this town. My heart was so warmed and encouraged by how the community had accepted her with open arms.

We made our rounds, Cara with her arms pumping, and headed back to her street. She tipped her head to the Gallagher house as we passed. "Come on. May as well be neighborly," she said. Since they were sitting on the wide, painted stone porch, we couldn't pretend we hadn't seen them.

"How do!" she called, making her way up the driveway past an enormous SUV, waving one arm like a flag flapping in the wind.

"Out for your evenin' walk, I see," said an older woman from her seat. Her gray-streaked hair was pulled into a tight bun. She wore a long and faded floral caftan and held a mug of tea. A saucer with remnants of cake sat on a wooden TV tray in front of her. "I've been watching the weekly numbers. If you keep it up, you'll beat Earline this month."

"That's the plan," said Cara, bending to tap her cheek to the woman's. "I'm taking advantage of her being out of town with the Colonel. I'm hoping they found a reason to be off their feet this week."

She stepped back after clapping the older man on the shoulder. "This here is my niece, Sabrina. Visiting from Atlanta for a while. She hasn't been out here since I moved from Healy, so it'll be nice to show her around our little town. Sabrina," she said to me, "meet my good friend Patricia and her husband, Cliff. They own Pinkney's, the neighborhood grocery. Pinkney's is where people shop the most."

I extended a hand and a cordial, polite greeting to Patricia and Cliff Gallagher, then stopped at the man seated in a chair next to them. He stood and shook my hand, introducing himself as Reid. Once I was up close, looking into warm brown eyes in view of smooth, flawless dark cocoa skin and a lush beard, my cheeks warmed.

He wore dark jeans, a long-sleeved shirt that didn't hide muscular arms or a chiseled chest, and leather boots that made me imagine him astride a horse for no good reason. A scar above his left eyebrow added character to his handsome face. I worked overtime to stop myself from staring.

Maybe Aunt Cara's encouragement about entertaining a rebound wouldn't go unheeded. Not that I would bed the neighbor's son...but if he was in any way representative of the men in Potter Lake, I would not be in a hurry to return to Atlanta.

"Great to meet you," he said in a deep voice as smooth as honey as he stepped aside. "Please take my seat."

At his mother's request, he left and returned with more chairs from the back porch. Aunt Cara and I settled around the crackling fire pit that sent the aroma of burning pine needles into the air.

"Reid, I'm sure your mother has told me before, but humor an old lady and remind me whereabouts you live?"

"Ohio, ma'am. Shaker Heights area, a Cleveland suburb. You heard of it?" At the negative shakes around the porch, he laughed. "That's why I live there."

"And what is it that people in Shaker Heights, Ohio, do for a living?"

"I'm a partner in a real estate development firm. We buy land and build whatever communities need for growth and innovation. Department and convenience stores, apartment buildings, shopping centers...that kind of thing."

Aunt Cara hummed, rocking her head forward and back. "I see." She glanced over at Patricia, then back to Reid. "You're not about to treat us like we're country bumpkins, are you?"

"I already told him to leave that alone," said Patricia. "No sense in unearthing that mess that Quincy was involved in. We don't need nothin' that takes away from the businesses that have always been here. We got a mayor that understands that, and I expect Kade will tell him the same."

My head swiveled to catch Reid's reaction. He shrugged, saying, "I'm here to visit my parents and make sure the house is sturdy, especially since there have been some fierce storms lately, and enjoy time off of work."

After surveying the blank stares, he dipped his head slightly. "Okay, and…if there is some land around town that is available, my company might be interested in development—"

"To which I say no, thank you," Patricia added. "But we'll see what city council says."

"Mama, you don't even know what I'm—"

"I know enough!" She snapped. "I know you blow into towns like ours, grab up land and start puttin' up big, ugly buildings that block views of nature, and take work away from homegrown businesses. How can you even consider doing something like that to the people in this town—some of whom have known you your whole life? Well, I won't stand for it, Reid."

Patricia let out a huff, then picked up her saucer of cake crumbs and stood. "Cara, why don't you come inside? I baked another pound cake and if I don't start getting rid of it, we'll eat the whole thing."

My aunt joined Patricia, chatting as they walked back into the house. Cliff slapped his knee with one hand and stood as well. "Welp. I got a cigar and some whiskey waiting for me on the back porch. Make sure you douse that fire before you tuck in for the night, son."

With a nod, he set off around the side of the house to the backyard.

"I'd like to say she's not always like that, but it would be a lie," said Reid. "I love that woman, but…" He paused, shaking his head. "I can't have the same argument about my job every time I see her."

"That would be intense if I had to sit through it every time I came to town."

"Yeah. Intense is a good word for it. She's all bark, though. Well, mostly bark."

Reid offered a halfhearted smile, leaning to the side to whisper conspiratorially, as if anyone else was on the porch with us. "My dad mentioned whiskey, and now I can't think about anything else. You want a taste?"

I was not much of a liquor drinker, but after the week I'd had, I could use a little something to knock the edge off. I nodded.

Reid left and returned with two mismatched tumblers of velvety brown liquid, then dropped heavily into the seat next to me. He clinked his glass against mine before taking a sip, nodding and licking his lips afterward.

"So, enough about me. For real. We didn't get around to putting you on the spot. You're here visiting your aunt? From Atlanta? For...*a while*? I know there's a story there."

I brought the glass to my lips for a fortifying sip. It burned so good going down. "Oh yeah," I said, almost choking. "There's a story, alright."

"If liquor gives you a loose tongue, I'm all ears."

Reid leaned back in his chair, all eyes on me. I shifted in my seat, heat rising in my cheeks again. I wasn't used to being the subject of such an intense gaze from a man who offered his undivided attention.

"I'm...*hiding out*," I began. "For someone who's prominent in Atlanta finance, my husband is a messy bitch. He's been cheating on me for some time. I thought I was being stealthy, making moves to leave him at the end of the year. But..."

I exhaled, releasing the tightness in my chest before taking another sip of whiskey. It was strong, but it was helping loosen me up. This was the most relaxed I'd been in months.

"He got caught. By his mistress' husband."

I glanced at Reid with my lips rolled inward and pressed together. He sucked in a loud, sharp breath.

"Oh, but there's more. There was a fight, and of course, someone recorded Adrian getting his ass beat. If WorldStar still exists, it'll be there soon. Adrian and I work for the same bank. I'm not sitting through meetings, pretending everything is fine, while people give me soft, sad eyes or corner me in the restroom with their stories and advice. So, I took some time off and came out to Potter Lake to stay with my aunt."

Reid gave me a sympathetic look. "I'm sorry you're going through this. But...you *knew* he was..."

I nodded. "I thought we'd be able to keep things quiet. One thing I need to do while I'm here is move forward with the divorce that I planned to file. And figure out what I'm going to do with my life. I've been married for..."

I fluttered my lips and shrugged a shoulder before continuing. "Damn near half my life. This is how it ends."

Reid gestured toward my tumbler. "I'm about to go get the bottle of McCallan. You're going to need a lot more to drink."

Chapter Three

Reid

A POUNDING headache roused me out of sleep before the scent of sizzling bacon could do the job. I sat up, groaning at the thump and buzz between my ears and swung my feet to the floor. The hardwoods were cold, so I played leapfrog with the area rugs across my childhood bedroom-turned-guest room to my suitcase and rifled through it for the small leather bag I traveled with.

I zipped the case open, grabbed two blister packs of ibuprofen and zipped it shut, stuffing it back in my suitcase. I plucked a matching leather toiletry case from the neatly rolled sets of clothing and headed to the bathroom. Since I'd be staying more than one night, Mama would grumble about living out of a suitcase until I gave her permission to unpack my things.

In the bathroom, I ripped open the pain reliever packets and swallowed the capsules dry, dropping the trash into the basket in the corner, then zipped open my toiletry kit. In the Gallagher home, we did not come to the kitchen table with unsaid prayers, an unwashed face or hands, or unbrushed teeth.

Once I was showered and dressed, with moisturized skin, my hair and beard combed, and pearly white teeth, I shuffled into the kitchen. Mama was at the stove, humming along to the Mississippi Mass Choir and Whitney Houston rendition of "Joy to the World" as she flipped pancakes.

"Mornin'," she said, glancing over her shoulder to peer at me above the thin frames of her glasses. "About time you got moving. I know you don't sleep late at home."

"Not usually, no, but I'm trying to relax for a few days. *Oooh*, bacon!" I reached to grab a piece off of the pile resting next to the skillet but thought better of it since my mother wielded a hot spatula.

"Mmmhmmm, that's what I thought. Go on and fix yourself some coffee and have a seat before you end up in trouble."

My stomach rumbled in anticipation. I kissed her cheek before grabbing a mug and pouring a cup of aromatic brew. "What's this blend?" I asked, reaching for the bright red bag. "It smells good."

"That's that Rooster's blend. I told you about Sage, the young lady who opened a coffee shop that serves that fancy stuff you need a machine to make—the lattes and cappuccinos and such. She sells the beans now, so you can take them home and grind it up yourself. We sell it at Pinkney's. It does well."

"Mmm," I said, after pouring a cup and taking a sip. "I see why you like it. It's nice. Kind of nutty, a little sweet."

"Nobody asked you for notes, Reid. It's coffee."

It was hard to tell unless you knew her, but my mother was having a ball. I smiled to myself and took my mug to the table, pulling a chair out to sit. "Where's Dad?"

"Out checking on his garden. There's a frost blowing in soon. He's late pulling in the last of the harvest."

I nodded, taking another long sip. The coffee helped wake me up and took the edge off of my hangover. Dad burst through the back door with a basket of vegetables.

"Mornin'," he called cheerfully, depositing the basket on the counter, then leaned over the sink to wash his hands before reaching for a clean coffee mug.

"You must be outside your mind, putting that basket on my kitchen counters, old man."

"Settle down, Patricia. I'm going to have coffee with my son before I wash those up. You should pick through them and see if you want to keep some for canning. The rest, we can take to the stand when we go into town."

Pinkney's still operated a small roadside stand on the edge of town. Sometimes it was too much trouble to ride all the way to the store if all you needed were a few tomatoes or had a taste for fresh corn.

Their easy affection made me smile. After over forty years of marriage, they were still crazy about each other. I hoped to find that kind of love someday. I recalled last night's conversation with Sabrina about the demise of her marriage. It prompted a rehash of my short, tumultuous union. In seven years, I had reached impossible heights and unbelievable lows with Elodie.

I'd been so focused on ramping up Sterling & Gallagher that I ignored everything else, including my wife and our son. When I looked up, she had moved out, filed for divorce, and left town for bigger, better, brighter opportunities. I considered striking up an ugly custody battle, but we agreed to put Joshua first. He was excited about living in Atlanta and though Elodie, a corporate buyer, was heavily focused on luxury items and brand names, she was an excellent mother. Whatever made Joshua happy, we would work together to achieve it.

That left me heading into my twilight years with no one who noticed if I worked too much or came home too late or didn't eat enough. I had no one to hurry out of the office for cozy dates with. No one to dream about relaxing by the fire with, something brown in one hand and tucking someone brown up close to me with the other.

"Son, I set out some coveralls for you in the mudroom," Dad said. "And some boots. Can't be out in the dirt in jeans that cost a hundred dollars."

"Whose jeans cost that much?" asked Mama.

"Your son," he said, sipping coffee while smirking at me over the rim of his mug. "They for sure cost more than the Wrangler jeans I wear. Can't have you getting those fancy threads dirty."

I chuckled. "Expensive jeans go in the same washer Wranglers do. I'll put on the coveralls before we head out, though."

Dad grinned and clapped me on the shoulder. Mama set plates, utensils, and serving platters of pancakes, eggs, bacon, and grits on the table, then sat down and bowed her head, extending both palms. As per our usual mealtime ritual, we listened while Dad uttered a few words of prayer, digging in almost before *amen* had escaped his lips.

The pancakes were light and fluffy, studded with melted chocolate and doused in syrup. I made appreciative noises as I ate.

"So, what's on the agenda for your first day back in town?" Mama asked.

"I told Dad I'd help get the last of the vegetables in before the cold front moves through," I said between bites of bacon.

"We're headed into town later on," said Dad. "You might stop by the store and see it—we've expanded, had the parking lot repaved and striped, got a big ole sign out front now. Looks real nice."

"The annual Christmas tree lighting is tonight, too," said Mom. "It kicks off the Winter Festival that the mayor's wife started. It's been real fun to see the kids and adults out there playing games, eating food, drinking hot chocolate. It ends with fireworks on New Year's Day."

I nodded, taking in my mother's message: Potter Lake was growing and changing organically and didn't need help.

"I planned on heading into town later. Might see if Sabrina wants to tag along. She mentioned she hasn't seen much of it yet."

Mom and Dad shared a look. I knew they were worried about my intentions. I didn't want to get into that conversation again, so I quickly changed the subject.

"So, Dad, you get out to the lake to do any fishing lately?"

Dad launched into a tale about taking Bennett, a recent transplant, fishing a few times. Bennett was dating Sage, the owner of Rooster's Coffee, which was in the same strip mall as Guys & Dolls, the shop that KC owned. I'd heard a lot about that shop over the past few years, and knowing he'd been drafted from our little old school made me proud. I had followed KC's illustrious career in the NBA before he retired due to injury.

His return to Potter Lake was surprising. I could think of a hundred places that a retired NBA player would rather live, and Potter Lake would have never made the list. I'd mostly avoided coming back. At the time I'd left, it was slow, dusty, and dying, but with Mayor Cavanaugh at the helm, the town was a vibrant mini metropolis with lots of appeal.

That wasn't a bad thing, I reminded myself.

Dad continued his stories about landing a huge bass near Sawyer's Point, close to the railroad tracks. I nodded at the appropriate times, but my mind had ventured off to my discussion with Sabrina last night.

Something about her made me so comfortable that we sat on the porch drinking and talking long into the night. Both my parents and her aunt had gone to bed hours before we decided we should get some sleep. Maybe it was her vulnerability and transparency, but there was something easy and unpretentious about her.

For the first time in ages, I'd enjoyed genuine conversation with someone. No business talk, no networking. Just two people connecting.

"Reid?"

I snapped back to the present. Mom and Dad were both staring intently. "Sorry...my mind wandered. Yes, sir?"

"I asked if you were ready to get in the garden. We can get in a good few hours of work before you head into town."

"With the neighbor girl," Mama teased.

"Oh, right." A flush climbed up my neck, but I refused to give my mother the satisfaction of acknowledging her comment. Sabrina was an attractive, funny, open...*sexy* woman. I was trying not to linger too long on the latter. "Let me get changed really quick."

I put on the coveralls and boots Dad left, rolling up the pants and sleeves, and followed him to the garden.

The morning passed quickly. We moved through the rows, carefully picking ripe vegetables and setting them in baskets. Dad kept up a steady stream of business talk and town gossip. I did more listening than talking, but I thoroughly enjoyed spending this time with him.

By early afternoon, we had run out of baskets, but the garden was picked clean of ripe vegetables. For the plots that needed more time, we used a few rolls of spun-bound frost blankets, driving stakes into the ground to keep the covers in place. We also covered my mother's bushes and flowers along the front and back porch.

By the time I stepped into a hot shower, my back ached. I was not used to manual labor, but I'd put in an honest day's work. After cleaning up and changing my clothes, I locked up the house, pushed my phone and wallet into my pockets, and walked next door.

Before I could knock, the door swung open, and Sabrina

stood in the opening in fitted jeans and bare feet. A pair of silver hoops almost got lost in her hair, which she wore in a twist out. The deep V of her gray crossover sweater dipped low enough to hint at cleavage and accentuated full breasts. I swallowed the lump in my throat and forced my eyes back up to hers.

She smiled, surprised to find me standing on the porch. "I was heading over in a few to see if you wanted to go into town. My Aunt is out and about. I guess she's right; I can't sit in this house for months."

"Great minds," I replied. "I figured I could give you the 'this wasn't here when I lived here' tour."

Sabrina grinned, her face lighting up. *Shit*. That smile was going to get me into trouble.

"Come on in," she said. "I need to put some shoes on."

I stepped inside and stood near the door, glancing around Cara Isaacs' home. It was…lived in, but not junky. Comfortable. Scattered among photos of her late husband and people I assumed were family were images of her with friends around town, some from around the state. At least one photo looked to be taken in Atlanta, and I recognized the vistas of Chattanooga, Tennessee, in another.

"Might want to bring a jacket if you have one," I called. "My dad swears a frost is coming in."

"Good call," she replied from another room.

Sabrina emerged from a room down the hall wearing a waist length-leather jacket and black Chucks, pulling a messenger bag across her torso. She smelled delicious… I couldn't help mentioning it.

"Whatever it is you're wearing, it's definitely working for you."

"Black Opium," she said. "It's my favorite scent. Adrian hates it, so I only wear it when I'm not with him."

"So…" I pulled open the front door and smiled. "All the time now?"

"Forever and ever...or whatever André and Big Boi said."

She laughed and locked up the house. As we walked to my car, I almost didn't recognize the sensation of being light and hopeful.

SABRINA AND I DROVE INTO DOWNTOWN POTTER LAKE AND parked at Pinkney's, where we got out to walk around. The square was busy, with lots of people ducking into and out of shops and restaurants housed in historic brick buildings. I pointed out landmarks from my childhood, like the old movie theater that was now a performance hall because the Cineplex, where you could order dinner and watch a movie, had opened the year before.

After browsing for an hour, we dropped in for a late lunch at Helen's, a breakfast and lunch destination in Potter Lake. Helen LeBlanc would cuss me out in English and Creole if I did not find my way to her restaurant. After a tearful, hug-filled reunion, she sat us in one of her favorite spots and set a basket of cornbread, rolls, and honey butter on the table. The lunch options were Salisbury steak and gravy, fried chicken, or meatloaf with the usual sides.

Over meatloaf, whipped potatoes, and green beans, our conversation flowed easily as it had the evening before. I could talk to Sabrina for hours and unless she stopped me, I probably would.

"I think you're being closed-minded about open air amphitheaters," said Sabrina, amid playful argument about the best concert venues we'd ever experienced. "The sound is better to me."

"The sound is *outside*. A few years ago, I took my son to see John Legend at Chastain in Atlanta. It rained the last hour of the show, and there's no shelter. John just kept playing!"

"Shut up, I was at that show!" she shouted. "I thought it was great."

"Even though you got rained on?" I asked, raising an eyebrow.

Sabrina cackled. "Even though I got rained on. That's the chance you take with an outdoor venue. Bring a poncho, wear waterproof shoes, have a change of clothes…"

She waved a hand at me. "You might be bougie, Reid."

"I'll own that. I want a seat and a roof and to not have to get wet to hear good music."

"I'm bustin' in here," said Helen, appearing next to our table to set a plate with a hefty portion of cake between us. "Y'all need somethin' sweet to accent all that good food. Reid, I remember how you love my praline Bundt cake. I brought you a slice to introduce to Sabrina."

"You spoil me, Ms. Helen."

"I haven't done my job if you don't have to roll yourself out of here." She picked up our lunch plates and added, "Say hey to Cliff and Patricia for me. If you need anything, holler," before walking away.

"I guess we're having dessert," I said, handing Sabrina a fork. "This is the best cake you will ever taste, and if you tell my mother I said that, I'll deny it."

After finishing dessert, we chatted for a while longer before deciding to walk off our heavy lunch. We made our way toward the lake, where the trees displayed a spectrum of bright fall hues and leaves were shedding in preparation for winter. The water babbled, creating a peaceful soundtrack to our steps. As we walked, I stole glances at Sabrina, admiring the way her hips swayed in her jeans when I hung back a step or two.

"This view is breathtaking," she murmured, admiring the lake at mid-afternoon. "I can't get over how everywhere I look, it's so…*picturesque*. Like right out of a Thomas Kincaid painting. No wonder Aunt Cara loves it here."

I was reminded, taking in the view of my hometown, of the survey I was supposed to complete and the changes I truly believed would revolutionize this community. I didn't want to ruin the afternoon with work, though, so I set those thoughts aside for another day. We talked and walked, lost in conversation, until the sun sank below the horizon, turning the sky a deep, dusky pink.

In the center of town, the square had been transformed into a lively winter festival. The crisp air filled with the aromas of hot chocolate, popcorn, grilled sausages, and boiled peanuts. Children shrieked with laughter as they ran from game to game, eagerly trying their hand at each one. There was a ring toss, lawn bowling with pins painted like snow-men, "ice fishing" with magnets attached to plastic fish and sticks to mimic fishing poles.

Booths stood side by side, boasting handmade crafts and tasty treats like taffy, frosted gingerbread, and varieties of fudge—hazelnut, walnut, dark chocolate, white chocolate. Before I could eat my weight in candy, Sabrina and I got drafted to a cornhole team.

After picking out a few painted ornaments, we headed over to the towering pine tree where a live band performed soulful holiday tunes.

Without the sun offering warmth, the chill in the air had a bite to it. I pulled my jacket closed and urged Sabrina to do the same, nudging her to Rooster's Coffee and Hot Chocolate stand. A couple was working the line, laughing and chatting with customers as if they were old friends.

"I'm guessing you two are Sage and Bennett," I said once we had reached the counter.

"We are," they answered in unison, with bright smiles.

"You don't even have to tell me who you are," said Sage, looking right at Sabrina, flipping the swoop of her bang out of her eyes. Her bright red Rooster's Coffee t-shirt peeked out from a puffy black coat. "Ms. Cara cannot stop talking about how her niece is here visiting. She was hoping you'd find your way into town. I hope we'll see you around more…and you dragged Cliff and Patricia's son out, too!"

My brows shot up in surprise. "Nobody needs an introduction in a small town, I guess."

"You look just like your dad," said Bennett, "so it's not at all necessary. Y'all want whipped cream on your hot chocolate?"

We headed toward the crowd milling around the tree with tall cups of hot chocolate and a generous dollop of whipped cream. I herded us toward the seats near a heater and waited for the ceremony to begin. My parents waved at us but opted to sit with their friends, a rowdy bunch of gray-haired people that included Aunt Cara.

"I guess we're not cool enough for them," mumbled Sabrina.

"Or…we're *too* cool."

"That's probably not true, Reid."

"Agreed." I sipped from my cup of hot chocolate, sending a band of warmth through my body.

Sabrina glanced at me, then glanced again in a double take. "Uh, you…you have some…whipped cream. In…in your…"

I wanted to ask her to lick it off but couldn't decide if she would welcome that request or leave me hanging.

"Do you mind?" I asked instead, bending toward her.

She hesitated before swiping her thumb under my lip. Her fingertips were cold, but the warmth that billowed through me at her touch took care of that.

"I look good?" I asked.

"Perfect."

The ceremony began with Larry Cable, city council president, opening the event in a brief prayer, followed by one of my favorite NBA players, Kade "KC" Cavanaugh, taking the mic. I fanboyed a little as he spoke, then introduced his wife

Leslie, who led us in counting down the seconds until he threw the switch that lit up the seven-foot Christmas tree.

As the tree illuminated, the crowd cheered, and the band started up again.

Sabrina nudged me with her elbow. "What a perfect tree! It's gorgeous!"

"Yes. Yes, it is," I replied...but I wasn't looking at the tree.

We milled around a while longer, but my dad's prediction of the cold front moving in proved to be accurate—the temperature drop became too much for our thin jackets to handle. Shivering, we hurried back to my SUV in the deserted Pinkney's parking lot. I started it up and turned the heat high, opening every vent.

Sabrina spread her fingers in front of the current of warm air, sighing in bliss as the heat circulated.

"Today was a good day," I commented. "Thanks for coming out with me. Definitely made it way more fun. My folks would have had me stocking shelves."

"Thanks for inviting me. I really didn't think I'd have so much fun in a small town, but Potter Lake is alright."

"Kind of can't believe I'm here now. I guess it's different if you're seeing it through fresh eyes. Or...if you're with someone you like spending time with."

Sabrina beamed a smile at me. My heartbeat ramped up double time. I was drawn to her in a way that I hadn't been in a long while, since before Elodie.

"Well, I'm happy I offer a different perspective," she said softly. "I really like spending time with you too, Reid."

I was about to sweat. I shrugged off my jacket as I looked away, pretending to be interested in something outside the window. This shouldn't be so hard—I was more than grown and had been on plenty of dates. Hell, I'd been married and divorced.

After a few minutes of silence, she reached across the console and tapped my thigh. "Was it something I said?"

I was on a road that diverged. Either I'd take the plunge, and we'd get everything out in the open and stop dancing around the obvious, or we'd agree the attraction was one-sided and I could stop wondering if I was the only one acting like a giddy teenager stumbling over his feelings.

"Actually…" I began, "I've been meaning to say this all day. Since last night, if I'm being real. I listened to you talk about your husband and all that shit he said about you and the way he's been dogging you and… I don't get it. I'm attracted to you. I mean, really attracted to you. You're… *dope*."

Her eyes widened for a moment before a smile spread across her face. "I…appreciate hearing that. Truly, Reid. Thank you."

"I mean it. I'm not trying to make you uncomfortable or anything, and I can take 'no, thanks, bro' like a champ. But I wanted you to know that we aren't all like Adrian. At least one man out here likes…*everything* you've got going on."

Before I knew it was happening, Sabrina was on her knees, leaning across the center console. Her lips landed on mine with such force that she knocked me back against the seat. I recovered quickly and responded with equal fervor, wrapping my arms around her waist and pulling her onto my lap. I had to move the seat back to make room. It was tight, but I made it work.

Her lips were soft and plump, her tongue probing as if she was searching for something. Sabrina moaned softly into my mouth, her hands roaming my chest before trailing down to the bulge that was growing harder by the second. I tucked a hand between her thighs; she shifted, grinding against my palm as our tongues danced.

I wanted to feel her skin, to experience her body responding to my touch. Tentatively, I played with the button on the band of her jeans and waited for a signal. She took the hint, popping it open and pulling down the zipper, guiding my hand inside. She whimpered as I ran my fingers along the edge of her panties, sensing the warmth emanating from her center. I began tracing circles around her clit, already growing firm against my finger. Her eyes fluttered closed, and her mouth dropped open. In shadow, I watched her face contort in pleasure.

I didn't dare stop, or slow down, or change a single thing…not as long as she was making pretty little sounds, crying out softly as her hips found my rhythm. She clutched my shirt, grinding with more desperation, her breath hitching as she moaned out in pleasure.

"Reid…" Her eyes popped open. She locked onto my steady, interested gaze and gasped, chest heaving. "You're… gonna make me come…"

"You better get yours," I told her. "Take it. I want to hear you come."

The way her expression changed when she came, the way her entire body shuddered, the way she tossed her head back and let a passionate, gut-level sound fly from her throat… I could never delete that scene from my memory.

She might have thought I was a voyeur, the way I sat there and watched her writhe, heave, and shake through the strongest orgasm I've ever seen a woman experience. In that moment, I wouldn't pull my fingers from her body if it meant saving my life.

When the orgasm subsided, Sabrina slumped against me, burying her head in my chest. "Oh my God…"

"Don't start, Sabrina. We're grown."

She said up and reached to turn on the interior light. "I've never…*please* tell me you don't think that was weird."

"I don't think that was weird," I deadpanned.

"Okay, now say it like you believe it and I shouldn't be embarrassed about what I just did."

I cupped her face in my hands, and brought her lips to mine again. "You weren't the only one doing things," I told her when our lips parted. "I don't think that was weird. That was the hottest shit I've ever seen, actually. You *needed* that."

"I really did," she said, heaving a loud, lung clearing sigh. "The other thing I need is to not be seen dry humping a guy I met yesterday in the Pinkney's parking lot."

"With the son of the owner of Pinkney's Grocery. Lord knows what this town would do with that kind of scandal."

We both giggled as she disentangled herself and climbed back over the console.

"So, uhm...how long do you think our folks will be out?" Sabrina glanced over at me with a quasi-innocent expression.

"No telling. My mother said this kicks off the Winter Festival. They might be out for a minute. But...we have a head start. And I know what I'm doing."

"Your parent's place? Or my aunt's?"

Chapter Four

Sabrina

THE CHILLY NIGHT air nipped at my cheeks as Reid and I climbed out of the SUV. He glanced at me, waiting for me to decide which way to go: his childhood bedroom in his parent's home, or my guest room at my aunt's house. I grabbed his hand and wound my fingers between his, pulling him toward Aunt Cara's.

"She's more likely to understand if she comes home early. And she takes a sleeping pill at night, so I can sneak you out if I need to. I don't even want to think about having to face your mother."

"Good point," said Reid, letting himself be pulled behind me across the yard and up the porch steps. The warmth of his touch sent shivers down my spine, in stark contrast to the dropping temperatures. It was cold enough to snow, an event that rarely happened in Potter Lake, or so I was told.

I unlocked the knob and the deadbolt to let us inside the house. It was cool and dimly lit. Aunt Cara left a lone lamp burning, so she didn't return to a dark house.

As soon as we were inside, Reid moved in, pressing my

back against the door. I gasped as his lips grazed mine. I gripped the lapels of his jacket, pulling him closer, deepening the kiss.

Reid's hands roamed my body, landing at the generous expanse of my behind, cupping a cheek in each palm, angling his hips so he pulsed against me. He was erect, hard, breathing heavily. Reid was ready.

And yet, he pulled back.

"If you decide you don't want this, say the word. If you're not ready, we can wait."

Waiting was the last thing I wanted. I was so starved for attention, for touch, for dirty, filthy, back-blowing sex that my body ached for him. The thought of not getting it was unbearable.

"I'm serious. If you want to take it slow—"

I laughed, cutting him off. "We don't have time for chivalry if you want me to be calling your name out before my aunt gets home."

I pulled away to lead him through the hallway to the guest room where I had been staying. The white walls and ceiling were bordered with broad bands of dark midnight blue. The queen-sized bed took up most of the space, leaving enough room for a thin nightstand next to it, a dresser in the corner, and an antique table draped in gauzy white curtains. On its surface sat a lamp with a frilly shade, an alarm clock, and a stack of books. Aunt Cora had made the bed with high thread count white sheets and pillowcases that were soft to the touch and covered it with a homemade quilt.

I tugged Reid inside and shut the door behind us, pulling off my jacket and letting it slip to the floor. The rustle of denim filled the room as we hurriedly removed our clothing, letting it lay wherever it landed.

In moments, I was nude…and so was Reid. I swallowed hard, my breath hitching in my throat as my gaze traveled the length of him, taking in his toned chest, narrow waist, and finally settling on nine inches of hard, veiny dick jutting out from his torso.

"Reid." I licked my lips; I could not stop staring at him. "I forgot to ask if you had condoms."

His eyes snapped shut, and he exhaled a hard breath. "Yes," he replied, bending to pick up his jeans. "But in my suitcase, not on me."

"You don't need to leave," I told him, holding up a hand to stop him. "I asked because I know men have their brands they like. But I have some."

I dove for my suitcase, which I hadn't yet unpacked because I hadn't decided how long I would stay in town. Zipped away in a compartment, a satin pouch held a few items I always packed when I traveled: lotion, lip balm, feminine hygiene products, perfume samples, and condoms.

"You packed condoms?" Reid asked, amusement riding his tone.

"Once I knew Adrian was cheating, I decided if I could… *explore*…that I would." I handed him the condom, still sealed in its pouch. "Opportunity is knocking."

"I'm answering," he said, plucking the package from my fingers. He ripped it open and had it rolled down over his shaft in seconds. With boldness, he gripped a handful of my hair and pulled my head back gently, baring my neck. He nipped at the vulnerable spot under my chin before soothing the sting with his tongue.

"Tell me you're ready for me," he murmured against my skin.

I gasped at the sudden change in his demeanor, but the take-charge attitude made me wet. My body thrummed with anticipation as I nodded.

No sooner than a shaky, "I'm ready…" fell from my lips did he turn me around, guiding me toward the bed. He moved in close, crawling up onto the bed behind me. Strong hands gripped my hips and pulled me up on all fours.

His fingertips dug into my skin, so hard I was sure I would see marks in the morning. I couldn't concentrate on that, though, because in the next moment, I felt his fingers circle my clit, using my wetness to prepare my body for him.

"Fuck, I need this," he whispered, holding me in place, working his way in until he could bury himself deep.

I hissed, closing my eyes, biting my bottom lip to keep from screaming at how good it felt to be full of him. He pulled me back against his body instead of letting me take control of the rhythm. I surrendered, letting him manage the pace. The backs of my thighs tingled as his thighs slapped against them. My grunts grew louder and more strangled the closer I came to explosion.

His strokes were powerful, masterful. If a person could be skilled at fucking, Reid was giving a dissertation on how to drive a woman up a wall. How did I let myself go so long—most of my life, apparently—without a good, hard fuck?

"Hold up," he said, slowing his pace and pulling out. I whipped my head around, already missing the sensation of him inside me. "It was beautiful watching you come earlier. I want to see it again. Flip around for me and lay back."

Happily, I obliged, scooting up on the bed and grabbing a pillow to shove under my neck. Reid hovered above me, lustful smoke in his eyes. I shivered in anticipation, but he disappeared. Seconds later, I figured out why when I felt the rasp of his tongue on my clit.

"Jesus! Oh, God…Reid!" I half-screamed when his tongue slid up and down my folds before he sucked my clit into his mouth again. I slapped a hand over my mouth to muffle sobs of pleasure.

"Spread your legs for me," he ordered, his hot breath sending goosebumps marching across my skin. "Give me some room; I'm not going anywhere. I want to hear how you sound when I eat this pussy."

The commanding tone inched me that much closer to

orgasm. I obeyed, spreading wide for the erotic assaults of lips and tongue. My hips began to buck and gyrate against his mouth. A powerful sensation was building to a crescendo, and I didn't want him to miss it.

"If you want to see me come again," I warned, "you'd better get your face up here."

A chuckle rumbled between my thighs as he kissed his way up my body. He stopped at each breast, taking a moment to suckle my nipples before pinning me with a searing kiss and filling me in a single stroke.

This time, when he pushed into me, it was like we were meant for each other. He was made to fit me. I was made to receive him. My legs shook with pre-orgasmic anticipation as he pulled back, then slammed into me. He repeated the movement over and over until he was fucking me hard and fast.

"You were so beautiful in the car," he said, urging me closer, "when you let me take you there. Can you show me that face again? Let me hear that sound again. Let me feel you grip my dick when I make you come."

I dug my heels in as leverage to writhe and buck against him. A delicious orgasm was so close, I could taste it.

"Take it," he demanded, not missing a beat. "It's yours, but you gotta take it, baby. Lemme see you come again."

I bit my bottom lip to hold back a scream as he crashed his body into mine. When I came, it was like nothing I'd ever felt before. My entire being vibrated, pulsed, contracted with the force of my climax.

Reid's head cocked back as a primal roar curled from him. Hips slapped against mine in a frenzied, wild, and desperate rhythm. He stiffened, convulsing violently before he emptied into the condom.

When he collapsed with a loud groan, my arms closed around his sweaty form. I welcomed the weight of him, hot breaths brushing my skin as we both slid down the hill of climax.

Reid rolled himself off me, grabbing my hip so I came with him. "So, welcome to Potter Lake. We hope you like our complimentary gift."

That made me laugh. It also took some pressure off and soothed away the awkwardness that I hadn't even imagined would come after having sex with a man I didn't know.

"Thank you for my welcome gift. It was exactly what I needed."

I yawned, looking around the room at the mess we'd made. Clothes and shoes were strewn everywhere, a condom wrapper lay in the middle of the floor, and the bed would have to be remade.

"Let's, uhm…not get caught in here when my aunt comes home. Do you drink tea?"

"Only if it has bourbon in it."

WE HAD CLEANED OURSELVES UP, DRESSED, RETURNED THE bedroom to its usual state, and gathered around Aunt Cara's kitchen table for a mug of tea—with bourbon—before two sets of headlights lit up the adjoining driveways in front of the house. I winked at Reid, who returned the gesture when Aunt Cara came through the front door, flushed red and cursing up a storm.

"It is *snowing* out there!" she said, stomping into the kitchen.

Reid and I hopped up to look out of the kitchen window. Sure enough, the lush green grass was covered in a thin layer of white, and snowflakes swirled in the air.

"Can't fucking believe it. It *never* snows here! Cold, yes. Snow? Shit, no!"

"Looks like Clyde was right about the weather for once,"

said Reid, staring out the window. "I can't remember the last time it snowed here. I think I was a kid."

"Maybe you brought it with you, Reid," said Aunt Cara from the hallway closet, where she hung her things. When she made it back to the kitchen, she eyed Reid and me. "You two left the festival awful *early*."

"It was freezing out there. All I had was that little jacket. I needed some heat, so we came here."

"Mmmhmm," Cara mused. She pulled a mug down from the cabinet and grabbed a sachet of tea, pouring steaming water over the bag to steep. "Well, I am tuckered out. And I'm not about to disturb whatever is going on here. I'll take my tea to my room. Enjoy the evening."

"Goodnight, Aunt Cara," I said with a smile. "We'll see you tomorrow."

She returned my smile as she headed to her room with her mug. Reid and I looked at each other with relief.

"I heard she has her finger on the pulse of everything happening in this town. Think we missed her radar?"

"Hmmm...no. She knows. She'll be full of questions in the morning."

Reid sighed. "That means my mama will be full of them in the afternoon."

I rose onto my toes to land a quiet kiss on his lips. "Enjoy your last few hours of peace."

Chapter Five

Sabrina

Morning rolled around much too soon, with bright rays of sun streaming through the blinds. I reached for my phone and unlocked it, then rolled to my back, pulling the quilt up over my shoulders since the air in the room was chilly.

I cringed at the number of hits on the *Adrian Ward* alert I had set up. I wondered if he still had a job, or if the board of directors at Aegis had already demanded his resignation. I made a note to text my director for intel. Divorce papers would be the least of his problems.

A text came in from Aunt Cara:

> I hear your phone pinging and dinging.
> Helen's for breakfast in 20 minutes! Get up!

I sighed, my eyes involuntarily rolling. Aunt Cara moved incessantly, maybe out of fear that one day she wouldn't be able to. She'd told me stories about Leslie, the mayor's wife, and her grandmother, who had lived at Primrose Gardens since her stroke. Aunt Cara volunteered there on Tuesday mornings.

She often sat with Grandy and read her the morning news. Her shifts at Primrose made her appreciate her own mobility.

Rolling out of bed, I tiptoed across the cold floor to the bathroom, then rushed through a quick shower, removing my scarf and fluffing the twist out that was barely hanging on. Aunt Cara promised to take me to the Curl & Dye to see if the stylists she was always gossiping about could do something with my hair. I was hours away from my regular stylist and, honestly, useless without her.

I coated my face in moisturizer, brushed my teeth, tamed my brows with gel, and added some lip balm to my lips before I threw on a pair of jeans, a sweater, and my favorite Chucks. I was sliding my arms into my jacket and coming down the hall when the door to Aunt Cara's bedroom swung open.

I always smiled when I saw her. She had such a peaceful, cheerful spirit, despite incredibly tough losses—first her sister, then her husband. After learning that she could not bear children, taking me under her wing since the day I was born made her the next best thing to a mother.

"Good morning, Aunt Cara."

"Mornin', honey," she answered. She reached over to fix the collar on my jacket. "Is this the only jacket you have? There's still snow out, and it's bitter cold. I doubt it'll melt for a few days. I thought Atlanta had cold temperatures."

"It doesn't stay cold long enough for a heavy coat. And I'm never outside this much. I used to take the elevator from our condo to the parking garage, then drove to the garage at work. What would I need a coat for?"

"What about shopping? The grocery store? Going for coffee? You know, things people do when they're not stuck at home or behind a desk?"

I shot her a playfully impatient look. "Please, Aunt Cara. We valet park at the mall."

She clicked her tongue and flapped a hand at me, mumbling something about lazy young people. I wanted to laugh, considering I was nearing fifty.

"You'd better bundle up," she said, turning to grab her purse off of the entryway table and motioning for me to follow her to her car, which was already pulled from the garage and huffing in place, heat vents on and seat warmers turned up high.

I glanced over at the Gallagher house, wondering if Reid was awake. Or, more pointedly, if he was reliving moments from last night like I was. From time to time, a flash of his expressions throughout the day—and night—would pop up. I also wondered when my aunt would make it obvious that she knew Reid and I had slept together. I was not looking forward to talking about what I'd been doing in her house a mere twenty minutes before she arrived home.

Aunt Cara navigated her Lexus through snow-covered, icy streets, past an array of shops ranging from clothing boutiques to convenience stores, all lit up with strings of white Christmas lights and festive wreaths. We passed a cute little minibus, which was also decorated for the season.

Apparently, we weren't the only people with the bright idea of having breakfast at Helen's Kitchen. The parking lot was packed, and the bustle of activity out front told me it was going to be busy inside.

After greeting and hugging half a dozen people, Aunt Cara paid for two breakfast platters and coffee at the front counter. She was zipping away her credit card when Helen LeBlanc walked through the swinging doors that separated the kitchen from the front counter, which was laden with sweets, miscellaneous fruit, napkins, containers, and plasticware for to-go orders.

"Well, hello again!" Ms. Helen called out. She was a tall, willowy woman with a wide smile and a voice that carried.

We couldn't ignore her if we wanted to. "How do, Cara! You alright?"

"I'm well, Helen. But what do you mean, *again*? I haven't been in here since last week. You know I come on Saturdays."

"I was talking to your niece." Her wide-rimmed gold frames balanced precariously on full, round cheeks as she beamed a smile. "She was in here yesterday, all hugged up with Reid Gallagher, lookin' really cute and cozy."

Aunt Cara slowly turned to level narrowed eyes at me. I returned her look.

"Ms. Helen, don't you start stuff. We were not *hugged up*. Reid said he would be cussed out if he didn't come in here for lunch yesterday."

"Don't worry about your auntie," said Helen. "She's just mad somebody had the scoop before her. Between Cara and Earline, nobody misses a thing around here."

"Where are we going, Helen?" Aunt Cara sputtered. "I want to sit down for this story my niece needs to tell me."

Internally, I groaned.

"Go on back near the window," she said, pointing toward the back of the restaurant. "I know you like that seat. Food will be around in a few."

As we wove between the closely packed tables, I was the star of the show. Heads swiveled to follow us, and whispers seemed to chase us down the aisle. I chided myself for pulling out a cashmere sweater and designer jeans to wear to breakfast. Where I'd probably blend in at a diner in Atlanta, I stood out like a sore thumb in Potter Lake. I wasn't sure if I could ever get used to small town scrutiny.

Once we were seated, Aunt Cara wasted no time. She leaned in, her eyes sparkling. "Now, I wasn't going to say anything because you're an adult, and I don't want to be a meddling old woman—"

"You? Not want to meddle? Did you not suggest that—" I

looked around, lowering my voice. "Wasn't a rebound your idea?"

"Sweetheart, I'm here to support whatever decision you make. But when we talked the other day, you seemed very much against the idea, so forgive my surprise. Seems like your mind changed the moment you met Reid."

I sat back while the server set two stoneware mugs at the edge of our table and poured coffee into them. She also left a carafe of cream and a dish of sweeteners. I grabbed two packets of sugar and flapped them together before tearing them open and pouring them into a mug, followed by cream, to lighten the brew to a beautiful shade. I lifted the mug to my lips and sipped a bit off the top.

"Sabrina!" she hissed, popping the back of my hand. I almost laughed at her octogenarian tantrum.

"What? What am I supposed to say?"

She huffed. "You are supposed to tell me what happened to change your mind."

"Nothing happened. Reid asked if I wanted to go into town. He showed me around. We went to lunch, stuck around for the tree lighting. We were freezing, so we left."

"My dear, I'll remind you that I am old, but my eyes work. One minute, you act like I've set the world on fire for suggesting that you have a little guilt-free fling. The next thing I know, I'm hearing from one of my best friends that you were cozy with Reid Gallagher yesterday. I saw you two at the tree lighting looking *very* comfortable. And then... *well.*"

Aunt Cara picked up her mug of coffee and sipped, before adding, "Your disheveled hair, chapped lips, and *afterglow* was a dead giveaway last night."

And there it was. I knew it was coming, but my cheeks were ablaze, nonetheless. "Aunt Cara, please..."

"What? I should lie? The way you kept looking over at

Reid, I would have figured it out even if I wasn't so perceptive. I'm only hurt that you didn't come to me to dish."

"When was I supposed to dish? After he left?"

"I was still awake," she said, her expression smug as she cupped the warm mug in her hands. "My bedroom is right off the porch, honey. That was *quite* the goodnight kiss."

The evening before, I had walked Reid to the door. We marveled at the sheet of unblemished snow on the streets before he turned to me and gave me a long, slow kiss that made my head spin.

"Alright, okay. I'm—"

"Do not form your lips to apologize or make excuses," she said, cutting me off. "You are a grown woman. I'm happy to see you smiling, having some fun after the drama and heartbreak of the past few months. Just, you know…" She rubbed a spot below her bottom lip with the tip of her index finger before finishing her sentence. "Be careful. You and I know what's going on here. Make sure Reid is aware as well."

I sipped coffee, pondering her words. I was on the brink of a divorce, on leave from work, my world halfway packed up and shoved into a closet in my aunt's home. My life was in shambles.

Reid was a handsome, successful man who had his shit together. In his presence, I was alive and sexy and desired. The attraction between us was undeniable, but he would not be the last man on the planet to pay attention to me. I could not drag a good man through the trauma of starting my life over while the entire town of Potter Lake watched like it was a new drama on The WB.

As if she were reading my thoughts, Aunt Cara tapped the back of my hand with soft eyes. "Don't worry about what people will think, Sabrina. You deserve to snatch whatever happiness you can right now. So long as Reid understands his role is limited and your…*fling* has an expiration date, I say go for it. What's that gal on the internet say? Treat yourself! Life is short, and you've wasted so much of it with a man who didn't value you."

I smiled weakly, grateful for her words of encouragement. I could always count on her to say the opposite of what my mother would probably say. That was why she was my favorite aunt.

She was my only aunt, but that was beside the point.

"I appreciate your wisdom, Aunt Cara. And your open mind. I'm mostly scared of what Reid's mother would say."

Aunt Cara blanched for a few moments. The light in her eyes returned when she saw a server approach with a tray. "Like I said, be careful."

Chapter Six

Reid

WHEN THE TEXTILE mill shut its doors thirty years ago, many families from Potter Lake moved to other cities. Some went to other states. The kids I grew up with had gone away to college after high school and, like me, never looked back. The best thing former Mayor Quincy Adams ever did was bring a crop of young residents to town and tie them to the community by insisting they open a business. Unfortunately, that meant there wasn't anyone around that I used to know anymore.

I was too young to hang out at the Kit Kat Lounge or the senior center, and too old to run with the younger crowd at Thai Bistro or the Cineplex. That left me bored and wishing I had already gone back to Ohio. I supposed it was time to get to work.

My mind drifted to Sabrina. Not that I could use her as an excuse—she didn't live in Potter Lake, either. That didn't stop me from replaying that night with her in my mind, from the kiss in the car, to the best sex I'd had in a long while, to the kiss at the front door. I remembered her soft, plump lips, and every inch of her body smashed up against mine. Although I wouldn't mind reliving that evening, I would understand if our time together had been nothing more than blowing off some steam. I enjoyed it for what it was...but I wanted to enjoy it again if the opportunity arose.

I started my survey on the older, historic side of town, where families like mine had been part of this vibrant community for most of their lives. The streets were dotted with charming brick buildings and row houses, but many of them desperately needed repair or restoration. Every store-front reminded me of the real people maintaining the character and history of this town. I couldn't and didn't want to disrupt that, but unless the town attempted to move into the current century, they would dry up and be left behind.

I scanned the surroundings, keeping my eyes and mind open to opportunities for commercial development. I paid close attention to vacant storefronts with faded "For Sale or Lease" signs hanging in windows. The architecture told stories of a bygone era, but the charm still radiated through peeling paint and worn facades. I noted the size and layout of each property, envisioning how they could be transformed into shops, cafés, or structures that would provide needed services.

On the other side of the lake, life was wholly different—I couldn't believe the two sides were the same town. The new architecture was flashy compared to the weathered buildings across the lake. It was also crowded, I'd noticed.

Business was booming...maybe a little too hard. With trendy spots like wine bars and artisanal coffee shops lining the streets, demographics were shifting. I pulled over to observe how businesses worked in this environment, hoping to find potential ideas that could cater to a growing demand.

I pulled back into traffic and continued my exploration, taking careful note of how much of a pain it was to access each location and the insufficient parking spots, if there were any at all. I paid particular attention to how close each property was to other necessary amenities or attractions and pondered the opportunities.

I wove through the major thoroughfare, the side streets, then each clustered neighborhood. Every vacancy held the potential to become a vibrant hub of activity for locals and visitors alike to gather and create fresh memories. My mission would be to find the perfect piece of land, one that would not only honor the town's rich history but also contribute to its future prosperity.

There were gas stations and auto repair shops, niche stores and convenient spots, but no McDonald's, no Walmart, no Target stores. Potter Lake had preserved its soul while embracing progress.

I pulled over next to a familiar grassy patch of land with a path that led down to the lake. It brought memories of summers spent swimming and fishing with my friends, of long bike rides and picnics with my family.

A shiny black Escalade with *TOWN OF POTTER LAKE* emblazoned on the side passed me. Abruptly, the brake lights illuminated, followed by reverse lights. I watched as it pulled in behind my vehicle, curiosity piqued.

Mayor Kade Cavanaugh stepped out of the vehicle, wearing a polo shirt and blue jeans that highlighted his athletic form. His long-legged, slow gait was reminiscent of his former days as an NBA player.

"Reid Gallagher?" he called out, extending a large hand.

"Yes," I replied, returning the gesture. "It's great to meet you, Mayor Cavanaugh. How are you, sir?"

"KC. And you don't have to call me sir, man," he said, laughing. "You're older than I am."

"Can't have you telling my mama I called the mayor by his first name."

"Your secret is safe with me," he assured me. "I heard

there was a guy walking around town that looked exactly like Clifford Gallagher. Thought I'd stop and say hello."

"I appreciate you stopping. I was—still am a big fan. You were a pleasure to watch back in the day, especially knowing you drafted from Healy."

"Yeah, coming back here worked out great for me. But, uh… I didn't stop *only* to say hi." I sensed concern in his tone and knew what was coming. "I know who you are and what you do for a living, Reid. I've had a few concerned calls already."

My head dropped, tucking my chin into my chest, but I was not surprised. There was no such thing as a secret in a small town, and I was living next to the megaphone. "I can guess who those calls have been from."

"Now, listen," said KC, spreading his arms, palms up and out. "I'm not trying to be antagonistic. Nor am I against progress and exploring opportunities to bring us into the future. I know you have a job to do. So do I."

He paused, splaying one large palm across his chest. "To put it plainly, I came to power because this town decided they didn't want to be overrun with impersonal corporations that seem more about profit than community. The people of Potter Lake will not be open to selling off land for anything that's going to leave a big footprint or change the landscape."

"Even if I didn't understand all of that, my mama has been going on about it since I got here. I'm not trying to disrupt anything good going on in Potter Lake. I came from here. Nobody understands Potter Lake like I do—"

"Well, now I have to question that." KC crossed his arms, leaning against his vehicle. "Most people here don't remember the last time they saw you. If you understood Potter Lake, you wouldn't sneak back under the pretense of visiting your parents to dig for information."

His words, delivered gently and without malice but pointed, made their mark and sank in.

"I'm well aware that Sterling & Gallagher has had their eye on property out here. Mitch Sterling is no stranger to me, and I've told him what I'm telling you now. If you think you're going to blow through here and squat something big and ugly in this beautiful little town?"

KC shook his head and smiled, but it wasn't a bright and friendly grin. "As my father-in-law would say, you've got another think coming."

"Mr.— *KC*... I'm here to stand between Mitch Sterling and my mama. Growth is a real good thing. Rapid growth, when you're not ready for it, isn't good at all. This town is sprouting up like a toddler in infant clothing. The population is outpacing services and conveniences. Look at your parking lots—"

I pointed out a few in view of the plot of land where we stood. "They're overflowing. Restaurants are packed, stores have a line out the door. And more is coming. Potter Lake needs more commerce to sustain growth, and more housing to sustain the population. A solution to that is what Sterling & Gallagher can bring to the table."

"Preaching to the choir, Reid. I was brought here to bring about the change you're talking about, but not at the expense of what we've fought to preserve. If you want to talk about building on what we have going and restoring what we've lost, let's meet. If it's anything more than that, you're going to have a fight on your hands, and I have this town behind me. Again," KC said, "I'm not trying to be a dick. I'm asking you to not be a dick in return."

"You have my word. I'm not trying to be a dick either. I believe we can come to an agreement that benefits both parties."

"That's all I ask. This town means a lot to me, and I won't let anything or anyone threaten it. That said," he continued, "to soften the blow, the town has a limited acreage of land it would sell for development, contingent on what it would be used for. We would be amenable to someone from this town taking the reins on that. Call my office. Let's hash it out professionally with my city planners, not by sneaking around and gathering information secondhand."

"Will do. Thank you."

KC nodded, gave me a two-finger salute, walked back to his Escalade, and drove off. I stood for a moment, watching as his vehicle disappeared. I got back into my SUV and started it up, headed to the store. My parents were expecting me.

As I pulled up at Pinkney's, I cursed aloud and swerved into a parking spot, then got out and jogged over to a produce truck, where my father was unloading crates and boxes from the bed.

"Dad! What the hell are you doing? You have staff to do this stuff."

"You yellin' like somethin' is on fire, son." Dad was soaked in sweat and breathing hard. "This ain't *stuff*. This here is work."

"You know what I mean. You hired people to do this exact thing. Why are you doing it?"

"They're busy. Checkout lines are long, and the manager needed all hands. I ain't working a register." He shrugged, bending again to slide a crate to the edge of the truck bed. "I do what needs to be done, and right now, this needs to be done."

I winced, watching the muscles in his arms tremble. I pulled off my jacket and tossed it onto a stack of boxes. "You don't think you're old, but you are. There's no reason a man your age needs to be hunched over and hauling heavy boxes."

"You might get your hundred-dollar jeans dirty," said Dad, smirking. "Grab a box, son. Many hands make light work."

We worked side by side, unloading stock, filling shelves, and storing the surplus in the back room. The familiar scent of my childhood filled my nose—a mix of fresh produce, toasty baked bread, and the aroma of coffee drifting from the café inside the store.

"Your mama's mouth has been busy," Dad said quietly, eyeing me as we loaded boxes onto a dolly and headed to the cold storage room.

"Don't I know it. Mayor Cavanaugh ran me down to give me an earful."

"You knew that was gonna happen. She really got a burr in her butt about your company buying land out here and got in his ear about it. Half the town, too. You know how news and rumors fly around here. Remember what happened to Quincy. You don't want to be on the bad side of this town."

Quincy Adams hadn't been seen or heard from since the day he lost the mayoral election a few years back. Supposedly, he had moved to an even smaller town in Alabama and worked his way onto city council.

"And remember, son, it's not always about the money," he offered, patting me on the shoulder as he passed me on his way out of the cold storage room. "Business is business, but this community is your family. You don't treat family like all they are is an open wallet to you. Decisions should benefit more than your bottom line."

I pinched my nose and tried not to sigh at my father. "I got it, Dad. Believe me, I got it."

"Good. Now act like it. Let's see what the café's got for lunch. Maybe we can talk your mama into coming out of the office to sit with us."

In the café, Ramona stirred a tall pot of Brunswick stew. Crusty bread was piled in a basket next to it. A pan of berry cobbler, warm from the oven, sat under a lamp to maintain its heat.

The café inside Pinkney's was intended to provide a place for folks to have a bit of lunch, but aside from Helen's, it was often the gathering spot. My folks and their friends had a table where they usually sat, so I directed Dad to have a seat and offered to get lunch for us. I set bowls of stew, plates of bread, and servings of cobbler on a tray and brought them to the table.

As predicted, Mama came out of her office to have lunch. I bent to drop a kiss on her cheek. She didn't shrink back, so maybe she wasn't still mad.

"You get all of your...*work* done?" she asked, her lips bunched up tight.

"Not really," I replied. I picked up a spoon and stirred the thick stew. It smelled delicious, and I was suddenly hungry. I tore off a piece of bread and dunked it into the au jus, savoring the warm and comforting flavors. "But...I got a visit from the mayor while I was out. He's not happy with me at all. Can't imagine where he heard about what *someone* thinks I'm planning to do here without waiting to see what unfolds."

"Ain't no cause to be sarcastic," said Dad before going back to his bowl of stew.

"Well, you don't seem to listen," Mama said. "Thought maybe you need to hear from someone younger. Or someone with more power."

I chuckled. Few people in town had more power than Patricia Gallagher. Not even Earline, the mayor's executive assistant, had as much pull as Mama.

"I heard what you said. And I heard what *he* said. Mayor Cavanaugh said the town has contingencies on the sale of land. If what we want to do fits within the guidelines of what they will allow, we might be in business. He told me to make an appointment, so I'll do that."

"*Hmph*," Mama huffed, picking up her spoon. She seemed more relaxed if I dared hope for a change in her countenance. "Don't forget where you come from. All I ask."

"Remembering where I came from is why I'm here. Trust me when I say you don't want my partner doing this work."

"We surely don't," said Dad, licking his lips. "Be runnin' back to Ohio with half an ass."

An hour later, I'd stocked shelves, swept the store, reorganized cold storage, and resolved an accounting issue that had Mama stumped. I was hot and tired and had not planned to spend my vacation working, so I declared I was headed home.

"We'll be behind you, directly," said Dad.

He looked—and sounded tired. For retired people, they worked entirely too hard for too long, and I wanted them both to call it a day. But I'd already learned that I couldn't tell old people what to do. I picked up a few snack items to take home and pushed out of the entrance, almost walking right smack into Sabrina on her way in.

She was as stunning as the day I met her in jeans, a hoodie, and boots instead of the Chucks she usually wore. She had a stocking cap pulled low over her head. Her face was buried in her phone as she walked.

"Heads up. You might walk into somebody."

"Oh, sorry," she mumbled, stepping around me. "Excuse me."

"Sabrina?" I called. "You alright?"

Her head popped up, eyes wide. "Oh, shit! Reid! Hi." She locked her phone and slipped it into the pocket of her jacket. "I wasn't paying attention. Long time no see."

She flashed a brilliant smile at me that made me weak.

"Hi. Uh...yeah. I've been lying low. Helping out." I nodded my head to the store. "Doing a little work, too."

"My aunt has been giving me an earful about Sterling & Gallagher. For her sake, I really hope you're not about to fuck up the vibe around here."

"I need to take out an ad in the paper to let folks know that's not what I'm about. There are some opportunities, though. I'm going to meet with the mayor about it, see if we can hammer some things out."

Her smile grew brighter, if possible. "That's great to hear. Ummm…" She paused, looking around to see if we had any eavesdroppers. "If I had your number or any way to contact you without standing on your porch or calling your mama's house, I would have. I had a *real good time* the other night."

The way her voice dipped low on "*real good time*" let me know how good of a time she'd had.

"I did as well. In fact, I was hoping to run into you to see if you had time or the desire for a repeat."

"More than I want to breathe air right now. It's honestly all I've thought about. I can't believe I've been going so long without…" I swear I saw her blush. "Anyway. My aunt has bingo at the senior center tonight. She's leaving around seven o'clock. If I get home with these groceries she sent me out here for."

She waved a short list, written on a yellow post card. "She's making a casserole with cream of chicken soup for dinner. Could…you find a reason to stop by around seven-thirty, eight o'clock?"

I was already inventing excuses to leave the house. I was a full-grown man, damn near fifty, and having to sneak out of the house to see a woman. It seemed silly…but I was teetering on my mama's bad side. The last thing I wanted was a lecture about messing with Ms. Cara's niece.

I pulled my phone from my pocket, unlocked it, and handed it to her. "Add yourself. Give me any info you want me to have. I'll reach out around seven-thirty and let you know I'm on the way. Cool?"

She took the phone, clicked through a few screens, and began typing. "I'm texting myself from your phone, so I have your number. Given all the mess with my soon-to-be ex-husband, I'm avoiding a lot of phone calls right now."

"Gotcha." I accepted the phone back and slid it back into my pocket. "See you later on," I said before stepping out of her path to the Pinkney's entrance.

"See you later. And Reid?"

I stopped and turned at the mention of my name.

"You should check the text I sent myself from your phone."

My eyes narrowed. I pulled out the device and thumbed through the sent texts.

> [Reid Gallagher]: You've never been fucked like I fucked you the other night. Get ready for a repeat performance.

"Just wanted to set expectations."

She spun on her heel and entered the grocery store without looking back, leaving me standing there with my phone in my hand and flashes of what the evening could bring in my mind.

Chapter Seven

Sabrina

GROCERY LIST IN HAND, I practically danced into Pinkney's, humming "This Christmas" by Donny Hathaway. Aunt Cara had been playing *A Soulful Christmas* on vinyl while running me ragged to finish decorating her house for the season. Then she decided she wanted to make chicken and rice casserole but needed a few ingredients. Of course, she couldn't go herself because of her *bad knees* and *achy back*.

I didn't believe those excuses for a second. She was spry and active and had reminded me many times that Reid's parents owned Pinkney's.

I didn't mind the errand. It was nice to get out and about. It hadn't snowed again but also hadn't warmed up much. The town had been in a flurry since snow rarely stuck around this long. Its presence made the Winter Festival that much more magical.

I wandered the aisles of the rambling country store, the warm air inside wrapping around me like a cozy blanket. I checked items off my list, mentally re-running that conversation with Reid. I couldn't believe I almost missed him, but I'd been texting—gossiping, really—with my director.

No one had seen Adrian in days. The executive staff were tightlipped about his future with the company. I'd been about to ask my director if he thought Adrian was drafting a forced resignation letter when Reid's deep, masculine voice interrupted my thoughts.

Nothing else mattered once I realized he was the tall, rugged person I'd almost run into.

It had only been days since we last saw each other, but the memory of that night with him made me thump. I'd spent so long—half of my life—putting up with subpar, *enough to get by* sex. Now that I was entering an era of freedom, I would not waste the chance to be stroked into oblivion again.

I felt renewed, full of vigor and boundless sexual energy. I also felt basic knowing that all it took was one extremely handsome man that paid attention to me to give me a whole new lease on life. I meant that text I sent. I had never been fucked the way he fucked me, and if that was standard operating procedure, I was first in line for another ride.

I rushed through the rest of my shopping when I remembered the ride I was looking forward to couldn't happen until Aunt Cara had made dinner, we had eaten, and she left the house for bingo.

When I got home, I found Aunt Cara in the kitchen, washing vegetables. "Find everything okay, honey?" Her waves framed her face beautifully as her eyes swept over the items I unloaded from paper bags.

"Yes. I got everything on the list," I confirmed, lining everything up on the counter. Aunt Cara returned to the sink after directing me to open two cans of Cream of Chicken soup.

She had changed the music while I was gone. The O'Jays' "Christmas Ain't Christmas" soared through the speakers.

The album had been a favorite in our household growing up. I wouldn't be surprised if it was my mother's record.

"I ran into Reid while I was at the store," I mentioned, nonchalant as we worked side by side.

"Oh?" She transferred the vegetables to the cutting board and began slicing the knife through them with chef-like precision. "Patricia told me she had a long list of tasks for him. I hoped you would see him."

"Aunt Cara, you're a sly one."

"Can't get a thing past my brilliant niece." She chuckled softly, chopping away. "Pull out my white CorningWare baking dish. It's in the cabinet next to the stove. And get that chicken ready to rinse before I season it up."

I set the dish on the stove and unwrapped the package of chicken breast, discarding the Styrofoam mold it sat in.

"So, what time did you tell Reid I was leaving this evening?"

I froze with a cold, limp chicken breast in hand. "What?"

"Well, I made it a point to tell you I was leaving for bingo tonight, and I sent you up to Pinkney's knowing you would run into him. Don't tell me you didn't take advantage of that massive coincidence."

"Of course, I did." I shrugged a shoulder and added in a mumble, "I thought I was being sneaky."

"I am a *meddlesome* old woman, aren't I?"

A prickly warmth crept up my neck at her words, realizing she had set me up. "Thanks, Aunt Cara," I murmured. "I told him you were leaving around seven o'clock if he wanted to come over. He's going to call me about seven-thirty, I guess to let me know if he can get past Patricia."

"Oh, I'll do you one better. I'll see if they're coming to bingo tonight. It's a cash game, and Earline is still out of town, so there's a better chance at winning. Not that we don't love that old bat, but it's nice when people aren't obliged to let her win everything because she works for the mayor."

Nerves and excitement about my impending evening plans shot up like a rocket.

Aunt Cara seasoned the chicken cutlets well, then laid them in the baking dish. She covered them with chopped vegetables and poured the cans of soup on top.

"Was Uncle Garth a flirt, Aunt Cara?" I asked, watching her mix and swirl the ingredients together, then slide the dish into the oven.

"Was he ever!" she exclaimed, her eyes sparkling. "Your Uncle Garth had the most charming smile and the prettiest set of white teeth you ever saw. He was our mailman, remember? He'd always come by the house, stop, and talk a few minutes."

Aunt Cara' eyes misted as she stepped into the past. "After a while, he started bringing me flowers. A little trinket here and there. That's how the young folks dated back then. Courting. Slow and steady, not hot and heavy like the kids do today. I swear, I get dizzy listening to them in the salon."

"But you still listen," I quipped.

"I enjoy all love stories, honey. Just because it's fast doesn't mean it's not love. Oh, I remember our first date like it was yesterday. He took me to a jazz club in Healy. What was it called?"

Her brow furrowed. "Somebody's Juke Joint. They wanted to bring Beale Street home, they said. One of his friends played in the band and got us in. We danced the night away. By the end of the evening, he asked me to be his girl and, of course, I said yes. The next fifty years were such wonderful, happy years."

"Sounds beautiful," I said, smiling at her story. Aunt Cara had always been such a romantic. And no wonder... Her Prince Charming was the most perfect man. I missed Uncle Garth fiercely.

"It really was. I wish—"

The doorbell rang, the melodic chime echoing through the

house. Aunt Cara set down her wooden spoon and wiped her hands on her apron.

"Now who is this, ringing the doorbell?" she wondered aloud. "Most people just walk in."

I started cleaning up the kitchen while she answered the door. I heard a male voice greet her, which made me curious, so I joined her. The man wore a brown shirt and pants, sturdy black shoes, and a ball cap. He looked like he was cosplaying a UPS delivery driver, but there was no big brown truck. In fact, a compact electric car sat in the driveway.

"I've got a delivery for a Sabrina M. Ward," he announced, holding a clipboard in his gloved hand.

"That's me," I said, stepping forward and drying my hands on a dish towel. The man eyed me silently for a moment before nodding and handing me a pen to sign for the package.

"Thank you," he said as I handed the pen back to him. "You've been served."

Without another word, he turned and walked away, leaving us staring at the envelope, then at each other.

"Did he say what I think he said?" Aunt Cara asked.

"He said I've been served. Do not even tell me—"

I ripped the envelope open and removed a stack of pages. *PETITION FOR DIVORCE* was stamped in bold across the first page.

I would have laughed, but it was more infuriating than funny. Adrian had hired a lawyer, set out his demands, decided what he would and would not pay for, and filed for divorce before I could even get my bearings.

"Can you believe this shit?" Aunt Cara grabbed the stack and flipped through the pages, shaking her head so violently her earrings swayed with the motion. "After all of that drama and embarrassment, *he's* divorcing *you*? Do you want me to stay home tonight? Go through this with you? Should you call your attorney?"

I sighed, suddenly weary. "No. I can't deal with this right now. I'll call Gibson in the morning."

"Alright, honey," Aunt Cara agreed, patting my arm and handing the stack of pages she'd been looking at back to me. "Let's get cleaned up and ready for dinner, so you can be ready for your date. After this, a distraction will be most welcome. I'll call Patricia right now."

We returned to the kitchen, where I tried to put my focus back on the comfort food cooking in the oven. Adrian, I was sure, thought he'd thrown me for a loop by striking first. I sat through dinner, thoroughly enjoying casserole and stories of a long and romantic love affair.

In the back of my mind, I counted the minutes until I could be up under Reid, celebrating the shortened timeline to freedom.

A FEW HOURS LATER, I STEPPED OUT OF MY BEDROOM IN A LOOSE t-shirt and black leggings. I didn't want any pressure for the night to be romantic. I wanted time to chill with a man I was interested in.

Despite that, I'd spent more time on my makeup than normal and had even twisted my hair into a presentable hair-style. As he said he would, Reid texted around seven o'clock to report that his parents were getting ready to leave for bingo and would ride with my aunt. He would be over to see me soon after.

As I waited for Reid, I poured myself a glass of wine to calm my nerves. My heart skipped a beat at the knock on the door. I crossed the room, taking one last deep breath before I swung it open to reveal Reid leaning against the door frame with fire in his dark eyes. A tight black t-shirt accentuated toned muscles. Like me, he was casual in black sweats.

"Hello, beautiful." He smiled as he stepped in, toeing off a pair of black sneakers before enveloping me in a warm embrace that smelled of charred wood and spice. "Feel like I haven't seen you in forever, even though it's only been a few hours."

"Hey yourself," I replied, breathless. "Come on in."

"You good?" he asked, following me into the living room and settling into the couch next to me. "You seem... I mean, I don't know you to know you seem weird, but—"

"But I seem weird?" I laughed. "It's been an interesting afternoon. I will be okay, but unless you want to hear all about my impending divorce, let's table that discussion."

He shrugged, his brows raised. "I've been through a divorce, so I know it's a rough time. People think you should be happy, but you actually feel like the biggest loser in the world that you couldn't keep a partner interested in you."

"You really know how to get to the heart of things. That's exactly what I'm going through. Like..." I shifted to face him, tucking a leg up under me. "I wanted it. I wanted to file first. To stand my ground, to appear strong. I wanted to hurt him, I guess. But this afternoon, Adrian had me served."

Reid's eyes looked as though they were about to fall out of his face. "He...already? *He* filed. After..."

I nodded, rocking my head back and forth. "After the fist-fight with his mistress' husband, the viral video, the embarrassment...all of it. *He* filed."

"He's not even begging you to take him back. So now it's like he's rejecting you again?"

"You missed your calling in psychology," I told him.

"Nah. I told you, I've been here before. I've been through therapy, questioning myself, healing. A lot of feelings. A lot of sowing my oats because I missed out on that, being married for so long."

"Mmmmm," I hummed, sliding closer to him on the couch. "And now we've come upon the reason for your visit."

"I mean...yes." Were he not so dark complected, he would

be blushing. I saw it in his expression. "Because you made it clear that you were open to it. But also, I really enjoy your company. If nothing happens between us tonight, I'll be happy to hang, talk, drink, eat. Whatever you're in the mood for. I just want to be in the same room."

"That's sweet. But let me tell you something, Reid Gallagher." I moved to my knees, swinging my legs over his body to settle on his thighs. "If you walk out that door and I have not experienced so much as a sniff of dick, you will never again know peace. I will hunt you down, brother."

"A sniff of dick?" Reid's chuckle was sinfully low, his hands instinctively wrapping around my waist. "I've never heard it phrased that way before."

"Get to know me. You might hear a few things you've never heard before."

I leaned in, closing the distance between us with a soft kiss that quickly deepened. A familiar flutter traveled through my body, culminating in a searing heat building at my core. His hands traveled under the hem of my t-shirt, pushing it up until my breasts, encased in a sports bra, were in full view. I threw my head back and groaned aloud as his thumbs zeroed in on erect nipples while his lips kissed the generous orbs above the nylon fabric.

I rocked on his lap, relishing in the throbbing heat between us. Reid writhed in response, moving his hands to grip my hips and pull me in close so he could grind into me.

"I've been craving this all day," he whispered, his teeth lightly nipping me through the fabric. "Since I left here the other night, to be real. Pictured you here, close to me. Everything hard, standing on end. Wanting me like I want you."

I pulled him in for another lusty kiss before I leaning back to catch my breath. "Tell me you brought your own condoms this time."

"I brought my own condoms this time," he said with a laugh. "I don't know how long we have tonight, and I don't want to waste any time that you could be naked and up under me."

My mouth watered at the thought of his hands on my bare skin, his tongue rasping taut nipples, his fingertips grazing my clit...him stroking me deep. In seconds, I had crawled off his lap and stood, grabbing his arm to pull him down the hall to my bedroom.

As soon as the door slammed closed, Reid pulled off his shirt. His chest, abs, and arms were perfectly sculpted under the light of my bedside lamp. My palms itched to touch him, and I didn't deny them the pleasure. I let them travel over his chest, and down his body until I reached the band of his sweats. I tucked my fingers under the elastic and pulled, revealing a pair of tight boxer briefs holding his erection at bay. He did me the favor of yanking them both down, his dick bouncing between us like the most tempting piece of candy.

Reid grabbed me by the waist and lifted me up to bring my body flush against his own. My legs wrapped around his torso. He carried me the few steps from the door to the bed, where I let out the most satisfying moan into his mouth as he lowered me onto my back.

With a tug, he pulled my leggings and panties down over my hips, not even waiting until they were off to close his lips around my clit and lick me like ice cream on a summer day.

"Holy shit," I whispered, fisting the quilt on the bed and kicking my legs to free them from the fabric that bound them. My hips rolled under his power while I unabashedly begged for more.

He answered my plea by pushing his tongue deep inside my pussy.

"Oh—*God!*" I groaned, hearing my voice harmonizing with the pleased sounds from between my thighs.

He flicked and licked and sucked, sending rays of electric shocks through my body. My toes curled; my body convulsed in a pleasure so extreme that I was weightless. I cried out again as I bucked wildly against the pull of his lips and tongue. It didn't take long at all before that familiar tightening of my muscles began.

"Don't come yet," he said. "Hold out for me."

"Fuck you," I replied, laughing. "Did I mention that I've been dry since—*shit*!" I screamed as he nibbled my clit. "Reid, for real. If you don't put a *damn* condom on…"

He laughed, pulling back to pick up his sweats and dig through the pockets.

I watched through half-lidded eyes as Reid pulled a condom out and tore it open, preparing to take me in a way I had been craving for days. When he was ready, he resumed his spot between my thighs and spread my knees farther apart. I licked my lips and watched as he balanced and guided himself to me, entering me in a few strokes.

I kissed him hard, pulling hm close to me so he was in position to go deep. His strokes were slow, long, and full of a carnal appreciation I could have only dreamed of, because I had certainly never experienced it before now.

This wasn't the sex of a one-night stand or the desperation of a woman on the rebound. It was not lost on me that this moment with Reid was the closest I had ever come to making love.

Reid drove into me, pinning me to the bed. I gripped his ass and bucked to meet the pounding thrusts of his hips against mine.

"Damn, girl," he hissed into my ear. "I'm trying to give you more than a taste, but you got me in a vice grip."

"I'm here for a good time, not a long time. Make me come."

"Tell me what you want. Come get it."

"Fuck me so good that I ache tomorrow," I whimpered. "Make me come so hard I black out. I want to be seeing stars and shit."

Reid chuckled. "That's a lot of demands."

"You said to tell you what I want."

"And I'm listening. Let me see what I can do."

"You're coming with me, right?"

Reid smiled down at me, still buried deep. "Hell, yeah. Take me with you, sexy."

He resumed steady thrusts, but now there was an urgency behind them. Our bodies moved in perfect rhythm as he plunged fast and fierce, so powerful that my breasts bounced each time his body connected with mine.

"God*damn*," he groaned. "Feel so fucking *good*!"

As much as I wanted to compliment the strength of his body, the depth of his stroke, his competency in driving me to heights I had never experienced, I no longer had breath or brain function. I could only grunt so hard and loud that my throat was sore.

The world disappeared around us; there was only Reid and me, locked in an intense moment of pure ecstasy. Our rising moans of approaching climax, the thump of the headboard against the wall as the bed rocked with our movements, and the slap of skin against skin drove me higher.

"Shit! Comin'!" I heard, a moment before my orgasm hit like a freight train.

"Reid!" My muscles tensed and released in rapid succession as my back arched up off the bed. He kept moving, his body grinding into mine, riding through my climax and prolonging the pleasure until we collapsed, falling into each other.

Reid's body weight on top of me offered the comfort of a security blanket. Our heavy, labored pants slowed to a regular rhythm. We lay there for a few moments, while our minds returned to earth.

He shifted so he laid next to me. I followed, rolling toward him, letting him pull me close and wrap his arm around me. I snuggled into him, exhausted and exhilarated.

"So…you see any stars or anything?" He asked, breaking the silence.

I burst into laughter, smacking his sweaty skin with my palm.

"What would you rate that? Like a nine? Ten?"

"Twelve," I answered. "That was exactly what I needed."

"Glad to be of service."

I propped myself up on one elbow, reaching to trace the scar on his face. "I've been wondering…what's this scar from? I don't mean to stare at it, but it catches my eye."

A half-smile crossed his lips. "Got clocked upside the head at recess. If I remember right, it was a baseball. I think I was… eleven? Twelve? It bled like a bitch. My mama thought I was dying. Doc Moore can't stitch a cut to save his life."

"Well, the scar is sexy," I muttered, my fingers following the ridge. "Uhm…so, I hate to bring up my aunt at a time like this, but she wanted me to make sure we were on the same page. You know, about…"

"About us sleeping together? She wants to make sure I don't catch feelings? Take you away to Shaker Heights, Ohio?"

"Something like that. I need to be clear that I like this. I need this, especially on a day like today, when my husband kicked me in the face…*again*. But—"

"That's all it is," he finished. "Satisfying a need. A want. I'm there too. I haven't had time for anything close to sex in the last two years. This has been a nice outlet."

"Okay. So, we're not going to have a huge issue when you leave town? Or…when I do?"

"Nah," he said, pursing his lips. "Not from me, anyway. When are you leaving town?"

I relaxed again, laying my head against his chest. "I have no idea. I have to go back to the real world eventually, but my director said to take as much time as I need. I have a good team that's doing fine covering the gaps. But if Aegis doesn't fire Adrian…"

"Ain't no way you can still work there after he embarrassed you and himself, then filed for divorce."

"Right. I'm thinking past January first. What about you?" I asked, tipping my head up to see him. "When are you leaving?'

"I won't know until after I meet with KC and see what's up with this land situation. He's talking like the city has some plots up for grabs, but with a heavy stipulation on them. The contingencies might make developing here a non-starter. I hope he wouldn't invite me to a meeting just to put up a bunch of roadblocks."

"From what my aunt says, he's not against bringing in new businesses and building up the town. He's not looking for anything…"

"Big," Reid finished. "So, nothing nationwide. No chains. Nothing you can find in Healy. Or Atlanta. Or Shaker Heights."

"Exactly. Will your partner be okay if you can't put some big corporation out here?"

"I'll be honest, Sabrina. The idea that I would come out here and tear this place apart…" He shook his head. "That's not what we're about. I know that's what my mother thinks we do, but it's not. We want to play a hand in helping small towns help themselves. Parts of this town will fade away in a few years if they don't do something."

"That doesn't mean build a big store," I said. "Especially one that puts your folks and their friends out of business."

"You're right. I'm not trying to do that, but if it means the town survives another fifty years, I have to present that option."

"I don't envy you, Reid. I would totally bury my head in the sand."

I felt his laughter rumble through his chest. "I've been

trying to, but Mitch threatened to come out here himself. He's smart, motivated, kind of a genius...but he's really annoying. I don't want my favorite NBA player to have to send him packing. And I don't want my mother to meet him."

I couldn't help but laugh at that. I barely knew Reid's mother, but I could easily envision the sharpness of her tongue.

"Not to change the subject," Reid said, "but this house smells damn good, and I've worked up an appetite. Did you and Ms. Cara have any casserole left over?"

Chapter Eight

Reid

Mayor Kade Cavanaugh's suite at City Hall was nice, but less opulent than I imagined a mayor's office would be. It was spacious and well-furnished, but it lacked the excessive grandeur I had come to associate with politicians.

The reception desk, like everything else in the office, was neat and organized. A gold nameplate read *Earline Myers-Lloyd, Executive Assistant*. My brows rose in recognition of the name that fell from my mother's lips at least once a week. A large corkboard hung on the wall behind the desk, covered with various pictures, newspaper clippings, and other colorful items that gave the office a casual, homey air. Some showed KC with his family, others with residents at community events. There were even a few candid shots of him playing basketball with kids at an outdoor court. It was clear that he was involved in the town and its people.

"Oh, hi!" A voice echoed from down the hall, accompanied by the rhythmic clack of heels on the polished hardwood floors.

My mother told me that the building used to be headquarters for Carney Carpet Manufacturing. The interior had been remodeled and updated, but the floors were original and well cared for. As I turned to face the source of the voice, I was met with a woman wearing a long-sleeved sweater dress and boots. Her locs cascaded down past her shoulders. Her smile was wide and practically warmed the room.

I recognized her right away as Leslie, the mayor's wife and owner of The Curl & Dye. My mother had sent photos of their impromptu wedding at the Kit Kat Lounge, held a few months after KC was elected.

"I'm so sorry," said Leslie. "Kade's assistant is on vacation and I'm pulling double duty. I meant to be out here to greet you. You probably don't remember me, but I'm—"

"Leslie." I reached out to take her hand in both of mine and returned her smile. "I was pretty far ahead of you in school, but of course I know the name. Ms. Lee gave me all my haircuts until I moved away. Please accept my very late congratulations on your wedding and the birth of your son."

"Thank you!" She beamed, walking to the desk to pick up a gold frame. The boy in the photo was a carbon copy of KC and looked like a natural holding a basketball. "Kade Junior, or KJ, is three years old, talking his grandparents' ears off, and growing like a weed."

"Handsome young man, there," I commented. "He's tall for three. Think he'll take after his dad?"

"In every way. A showboat that likes candy, is never afraid of a camera, and is best friends with a basketball." She laughed and set the photo back on the desk, careful to arrange it just so. "Earline does not like me to mess with her things. Let's head this way, so we don't get into more trouble. KC is finishing up a breakfast meeting."

In KC's office, a mahogany desk sat in front of curtained windows. Two guest chairs were placed in front of the desk and bookcases flanked the windows that showcased an amazing view of the lake and the other side of town, surrounded by the lush green of forest. On the other side of the office was a casual grouping of couches and chairs around a low, wide coffee table. A few magazines, some weathered with KC on the cover, were piled in the center of the table. On the walls, among a few plaques, his degrees, and photos, were framed posters showcasing KC in the uniforms of every team he had played for. An open door hinted at a private conference room with a meeting table and chairs.

Leslie led me to the waiting area and invited me to make myself comfortable, taking a seat opposite me. "Are you enjoying your visit home? Ms. Patricia was beside herself once she knew you were coming down for a few weeks."

"It's been really nice to be home," I admitted, surprising myself by being genuine. The tension between my mother and me was nothing new; I frequently skirted around work topics because she was sensitive to gentrification and pushing people out of homes and businesses, despite my repeated attempts to educate her on what my actual role at Sterling & Gallagher encompassed. Even with our communication difficulties, she liked to spoil me, and it had been a very long time since I'd had Patricia Gallagher's good cooking. I would return to Ohio with a few pounds to take off, for sure.

"How long are you planning to be in town? The festival has been a big hit in recent years. I saw you at the Tree Lighting the other night. There will be something fun every week to bring the community out, and we always do fireworks for the New Year."

"I'm not exactly sure," I replied, leaning back into the plush cushions of the couch. "It really depends on what KC and I discuss today, but I'm hoping to stay for a little while longer. I honestly avoided Potter Lake for so many years and I'm regretting it. It's nice to see how things have changed."

Leslie nodded in agreement, her eyes scanning the room from the photos on the wall to the view outside the windows. "I'm proud of KC. He worked hard to gain the trust of the people here, and in return, he's done so much for them. He's brought in new businesses, help establish public transportation, fought for funding from the state for streetlights, started up community organizations."

"I can see that," I said. "And it's good to hear."

"For example," she continued, "his breakfast meeting is about expanding the bank. The community needs way more services than it used to, which means organizations have to step up to the plate to provide them. He's trying to update some of the older areas of town. Even the residents that were against such things when Mayor Adams was in office seem to be coming around now that KC is here doing the work."

"I see you, going to bat for this town," I said, "and let me be the first to tell you that I get it. There are a lot of rumors flying around about why I'm here. I had a good conversation with KC the other day about getting down to real business. Helping, not hurting. Expanding, not closing. Building, not tearing down."

"I have heard the rumors, yes." Leslie nodded. "And yes, I champion this community. I ran away the first chance I got, too. But this town was here when I needed a soft place to land. It was here for KC, too. It brought us back together and gave us a life we never imagined. I can't stand to think about someone coming in here to turn it into another Healy. Or Atlanta."

She shuddered, and probably not involuntarily. "My heart is a little lighter, though, hearing this right from you. KC will make sure you stick to that."

I chuckled, enjoying the easy conversation. "Indeed, he will."

The thump of heavy footsteps sounded in the hallway. Leslie pushed herself up from the chair. I stood as well, following her to meet him at the door.

KC walked in, dressed down in slacks that appeared tailored to fit his frame and a polo shirt with *TOWN OF*

POTTER LAKE embroidered on the left breast pocket. He carried a folio in one hand and held a phone to his ear. He bent to brush his lips across Leslie's, lifting the folio in a wave to me as he headed to his desk.

"Alright, Mom. Thanks for the update. Earline is on vacation, but she's back tomorrow. I'll ask her to cancel your flight and set you up on the train. It'll be good to have you in town a few days longer." He paused, listening as he dropped into the leather executive chair behind the desk. "It's not a bother at all. TC is ready for you. We've had all kinds of ADA updates around town, so I'm looking forward to you testing them out in your wheelchair."

His eyes flicked up at me. He smiled, motioning for me to sit in one of the chairs. Leslie leaned a hip against his desk, a wrinkle of concern forming between her brows that did not disappear when he insisted that he had to go and slid his thumb across the face of the device.

"They're canceling their flight?" Leslie asked quietly. "I thought her neurologist said everything looked good?"

KC sighed, pressing the button on the side of his phone and laying it on the desk. "He did. She's cleared to fly if she needs to, but she's nervous about flying with her new wheelchair."

"Mmmmm." Leslie shook her head, crossing her arms tight over her chest. "We just got her that chair. The way the airlines threw around her old one—"

"Right. So, she decided she wants to travel by train. You know, the nice, updated trains with the private room and fancy lounges at each station." KC rolled his eyes. "She saw some report on the news and looked into it. They have accessible seating in first class, so she can stay in her chair and move around as she needs to. They're all excited about a long ass train ride from Texas."

"Oh, they will love that, though." Leslie's look of worry melted as her smile spread. "You want me to call her and get the information? That way, you don't have to wait for Earline to take care of it?"

"That would be great, babe. I'd appreciate it. Copy me and TC so she knows when they're coming. She mentioned wanting to come a little earlier since she doesn't have her next MS evaluation until after the new year."

Leslie bent to hiss him again. KC reached out to tap her behind on the way out, winking at me. When the door closed behind her, he sighed, sitting forward and resting his elbows on the desk.

"When I tell you I'm so happy I came back here and found that woman?" He shook his head and pushed out a grunt of satisfaction. "I love the shit out of her. She's helped me give this town what they deserve. She loves this place, these people. So I do too."

I relaxed in the chair, resting one foot over my knee. I was happy I'd played it cool with my attire. Mama predicted what KC would be wearing, and I'd aimed to match with black slacks and a short-sleeved shirt.

"She was telling me a little about that when you walked in. I guess we all left and came back later to give back to a town that gave so much to us."

"You feel me. How's your visit home been?"

I repeated the answer I'd given to Leslie. KC seemed to puff up with pride when I complimented him on the improvements and changes to the community. I also repeated my regrets about not returning home sooner. I could have always been a part of revitalizing Potter Lake.

"It's never too late to start." He paused, a smile tugging at the corners of his lips. "My mind has been spinning since we talked. There are a few projects in flux that we'd love to get off the ground. I don't have the personnel to push them, keep them updated. My city planners are…"

KC pushed out a loud, frustration-filled breath. "Let's lay it all out on the table. Mayor Adams amassed a group of people that said yes to everything he proposed. So long as they got paid, they were good to go. The people that have been on staff here were all his age and older. My executive assistant does a great job, but she's a seventy-year-old newlywed married to a retired Army colonel. She should be off traveling the world or sitting on her front porch playing bid whist and drinking moonshine. I've been slowly bringing a new generation into my administration, but I don't yet have a person that does what I need done. What you do, Reid."

KC tapped two fingers on his desk, his eyes glinting with excitement.

"For example, my meeting this morning was about expanding the bank." The chair squeaked as he tipped it back and swiveled. "We've got two branches, one on each end of the old side of Potter Lake. The buildings are crumbling, the technology is older than I am, the hours are limited. We need major development to update those buildings, plus open at least one new branch on the new side of town. We've got requests for a housing community for families and young professionals that are closer to commerce with some live-work-play options. We've been trying to get these off the ground for a while now."

"Okay. Seems like the previous administration had contracts with developers, but you cut all of those off when you took over."

"Well, we've been reluctant to reach out to Healy developers. They look at us and see dollar signs. They don't want to employ any local people. They want to toss up a department store, some fast-food joints, a few gyms. That's all Quincy was doing, and we ran his ass out of here. So it's funny that *you* should show up right now."

My interest was piqued. "I think I'm picking up what you're putting down."

KC leaned forward so fast his chair almost tipped over. "I've got land picked out—beautiful acreage. Easy access to the highway. What if we could do more with that land than put a bank on it? What if I put an experienced mind on this project? What if I roped in a homegrown, original son of this community to help us mold the land into what we want it to be? I'm not thinking about what could make a ton of money, or what would put people out of business and bring a traffic headache."

My heart almost thumped out of my chest with both excitement and trepidation as KC's plan swirled in my mind. Immediately, my imagination took over, planning scenarios and alternate concepts. I scrubbed my hand down my face, smoothing down the hairs in my beard as my brain clicked and whirred.

"Just planting a seed," KC was saying. "I want to see where you stand and gauge if you'd be willing to commit to something like this."

"Commit," I repeated. "I mean, when I think about this, it strikes me that this project would require long-range planning. A lot of time spent here. On the scene. In town."

As he'd mentioned, he did not have a person in town that he would assign the project to. I'd never turn this over to Mitch or install some lackey to run the project on my behalf. I'd never hear the end of it from my mother, and I could never do that to this town after gaining the trust of their mayor.

"This is not a part-time, every other weekend project," KC confirmed. "If you want some time to look things over, I'll give you the coordinates so you can check out the spot. Come to the city council meeting tonight. I want you to hear our ideas and open a conversation."

"If I'm honest, I'm scared shitless because my first impulse is not to turn you down." KC's brow hiked. Mine rose in solidarity. "This is a huge project, man. From the looks of it, you're asking me to relocate to Potter Lake for the foreseeable future. Do you have the budget to sustain that? Would I be working with silly string and paper clips?"

KC burst into laughter. "You've worked with small government before, huh? The bank is doing well. We have investors who are willing to put money into the project. We need someone to spearhead, someone with a vision to bring it to life. You can almost write your own check, Reid."

After a few minutes of conversation and reminiscing about KC's time in the NBA, Leslie knocked softly, then poked her head in. "Hey, babe, I'm headed to the salon, then my mom's. We're taking KJ to get an outfit for Santa pictures tonight. You have lunch with Kendrick to review updates on the city website, and your afternoon is blocked."

KC's grin was devious. "In other words, I have basketball league. A group of us all play hooky and pretend we can still run the court. You play?"

I shook my head. "Can't say I'm particularly skilled. I wouldn't mind getting some exercise, though. My mama won't stop making lemon pound cake."

"Who you tellin'? Ms. Lee has sent me a half dozen red velvet cupcakes every month since I started dating Leslie. You think I'm telling her to stop?"

He wagged his head. "So... Hooky League. We play at the rec center at four o'clock and roll right into city council. Super casual."

"Sounds good, man." I stood and offered a hand. KC took it and squeezed, giving me a few strong pumps. I almost winced. "I'll get out of your hair, but I'll see you this afternoon. Appreciate the invite and the vote of confidence."

"Don't let me down, Reid. Counting on you."

I walked out of the mayor's office with a folder full of research on a patch of undeveloped land between Potter Lake and Healy that would expand the city and provide room for growth.

This project would change my life if I chose to accept it.

Chapter Nine

Sabrina

"Oooh, I cannot wait to get in that salon chair!"

I gave my scalp a good scratch with my fingernails. A few sessions of sweaty, raunchy sex had done nothing to help me manage my hair. Beyond shampoo, conditioner, moisturizer, and hair oil, I was clueless. I'd been doing it myself...and my hair looked like it.

"Let Evonne work her magic," said Aunt Cara. She snapped her seat belt across her body, pulling on a pair of gloves that matched her black wool coat. "She'll be happy to play in your hair for a bit."

"She's the one marrying that guy from the music group, right? The Guys Next Door?"

"Mmmhmm," she hummed, pulling out of the garage and backing down the driveway. "Lovely couple, a sweet guy and gal. The group is on hiatus, and Taj is on winter break from his master's program. You'll probably see him around town. He works as a nurse in the clinic."

"A male nurse is...different."

"He's the best there is, they say. Very popular, and he's pretty much running the place. He and Doc Moore come over to Primrose every so often to help the staff do checkups and such."

I watched the garage door slowly close and glanced over at the Gallagher house as we rode past. The SUV Reid was renting wasn't in the driveway. That meant he was at his meeting with the mayor. Selfishly, I hoped it meant that it would keep him in town longer.

After my conversation with my attorney, my life was simultaneously the most peaceful and joyful it had ever been and in the most upheaval. Adrian had gone all in. He wasn't offering anything but money to walk away from the marriage. He petitioned to keep our city condo and our vacation home because he owned them both before we married. Under Georgia law, he was entitled to them and wasn't willing to give them up. He gave me everything in my name, half of our savings, half of our stocks.

As much as I wanted to fight for what I believed I deserved, I also craved freedom. Surely, there had to be more to life than serving as a trophy to a man who would eventually replace me. The idea of taking the money—which wouldn't be a small sum—and leaving everything behind to start over in the cocoon of a sleepy little town sounded more appealing every day. I longed to start fresh, to find a new purpose, discover new love.

If Adrian's deal left me free to experience everything I'd been missing with a sexy real estate developer with a charming smile and vibranium dick? So be it.

Aunt Cara turned into a strip mall and parked in a diagonal spot in front of a little storefront that radiated warmth and charm. The Curl & Dye was freshly painted in a bright turquoise color with a large hand-drawn sign above the double doors.

I quickly got out of the car and followed her in, buzzing with excitement at being able to walk around town without a scarf on all day.

"How do, y'all?!" Aunt Cara called, waving as she stepped inside. A chorus of voices called out in response, followed by a cacophony of laughing and talking over the sounds of holiday music playing overhead. Aunt Cara introduced me to the room, pointing out each of the stylists, then going to each chair to greet people.

I paused a moment to take it all in.

What Curl & Dye lacked in square footage, it made up in ambience and ingenuity. Every square inch of the salon was put to good use. A symphony of colors graced the walls, accented by vintage hair care ads, posters, and framed photos. Though it was cold out, sunlight poured through the large windows, giving the salon a cheerful glow. The stylist chairs were lined up against opposite walls. Each faced a mirror and a cabinet that held styling tools.

Across the back wall were three shampoo bowls with shelving above each one that held a collection of product containers. Up front, the waiting area was three plush chairs in a variety of earthy tones next to a wood reception desk. Behind the desk, a glass case was stocked with an array of hair care products, wigs, braiding hair, and accessories.

"Patrice! We have customers!" Tamera shouted above the chatter and music. A young girl rushed up the aisle from a door in the back of the salon. Her hair was styled into a short, silky bob with honey blonde highlights. The back was cropped short, while a bang fell over her face.

"I'm sorry about that. I got sidetracked," she said, sliding behind the desk and grabbing a pen. "Ms. Cara, Leslie is in the back working on your rinse right now. You can sit in her chair. And you must be Sabrina."

She glanced up at me with a smile so wide, her oversized tortoiseshell frames rode the roundness of her cheeks. "You'll be with Evonne today; she's the last chair on the right. She's finishing her current client, and then I'll take you over to her."

I set my bag down and leaned in. "I don't mean anything by this, but...who does your hair?"

"Evonne." She beamed. "You will *love* her, I promise."

I nodded, satisfied. If I was low-key planning to stay in Potter Lake for a while, I needed someone that could help me take care of my hair. "What's with the cabinet full of product? This town doesn't have a beauty supply?"

"We find it easier to stock and sell the products we recommend here. Also, Evonne has a popular hair care web channel and she get sponsors. If she promotes it, we stock it. She makes some money and so do we."

"Savvy. I like it."

"She's well-known because of her fiancé, you know? As soon as it hit the papers that Taj from The Guys Next Door lived here and she was his woman, people started coming from all over to get their hair done at the Curl & Dye. It's been wild."

She gestured toward the seating by the desk. "Have a seat and make yourself comfortable. We offer complimentary water, so grab a bottle if you need one. Zeke will come by later with snacks."

I sat in a chair and scanned the salon, the energy of the place seeping into me. I wanted to laugh out loud at this country ass beauty shop that I wouldn't be caught dead in last month, but I was too busy being mesmerized by how cute and homey it seemed.

My phone vibrated in my bag. It could be anyone trying to reach me... Adrian, my director, or Reid. After the tense conversations I had over the last few days, I debated turning off my phone altogether. When it buzzed a second time, I gave in and checked it.

> [Reid Gallagher] Just saying hey. Good meeting today. Gotta figure out how to play basketball— KC invited me to play on his league this afternoon.

> Also got an invite to city council tonight. Want to come along? Maybe we can find something to do after. ;)

I smiled while reading his message. Things must have gone even better than he hoped.

> I'm so excited for you!

> I hope that means good news. At the salon with my aunt. Should be back in time to join you tonight. Send me where and when.

> [Reid Gallagher] So I can't grab your hair anymore?

I chuckled under my breath.

> If you plan to grab my hair like you did the other night, you are welcome to do that any time.

> [Reid Gallagher] Been running that night back in my mind. Ready for a repeat.

> As am I... Can't wait to see you later.

> Yeah, I'll message you. These dudes about to run me up and down this court.

A distinct thump pulsed at my core. My temperature rose at the mention of his hands in my hair. I fanned myself, glancing up as I slid my phone back into my bag. I caught Aunt Cara's eye as a smock bearing the salon logo fluttered and settled over her body. She winked at me, then gave me a look that told me she knew who I was texting. She pulled an AARP magazine from her bag and slowly, lazily flipped the pages. I was lost in daydreams of what the night might hold when a voice interrupted my thoughts.

"Sabrina?" A woman with a flawless platinum blonde lace front wig and deep cocoa skin greeted me with a bright smile and a hand perched on her extended belly. "I'm Evonne. I'm a huge fan of your aunt. It's so great to meet you."

"Hi! Yes, I'm Sabrina. You're…how far…"

"*Very* pregnant," she finished, rubbing her belly. "She's almost here."

"Mmhmm, and you need to sit down somewhere," said Tamera from her chair. "I told Taj you would be taking it easy, not doing clients back-to-back without a break."

"Oh, I'm not in any hurry." I sat back down and pulled out my iPad. "For real, take a break."

"I'm fine," she argued, her gaze whipping back and forth between me to Tamera. "Honestly. Tamera—"

"Nuh-uh. You and baby girl have a seat for a minute. You need some water?"

"No, I'm good," Evonne said, but complied, slowly easing herself into one of the chairs beside me. She let out a small sigh of relief as she settled in and placed a protective hand on her belly. "I guess I'll take a quick one. I can brag to Taj that I rested."

"Thanks to me," said Tamera.

"Anyway…while we're sitting here, I might as well get to know you a little."

"Can we not pretend that my aunt isn't Cara Isaacs and she hasn't told you all how I ended up here? It'll save me the embarrassment of telling the story for the hundredth time and trying to make myself look good."

"Cheating soon-to-be ex, left town in a hurry, new lease on

life, et cetera. I was being friendly. So, what are we working with today?" She nodded at the scarf covering my hair. "I've seen it all. You should have seen Patrice's hair the first time she came in here. Leslie threatened to shave it off."

I glanced at Patrice, who bobbed her head in a nod. "Tried to dye it, then bleach it. It was *orange* and *crispy*. My grandmother was hot...dragged me in here. Evonne saved my hair. Now look at it." She ran her fingers through her spunky short hairdo and grinned.

"I'm sold." I pulled the scarf from my head to reveal a set of tired, dry twists. Strands of gray popped out everywhere. "Please help me. I'm used to sitting in a salon chair once a week. I'm lost without a pair of gifted hands in my hair."

Evonne laughed. "Girl, that ain't nothin' a good hydrating wash and deep conditioner can't fix. I use a shea butter mix that'll give you some longevity and moisture. I also sell a satin-lined bonnet to sleep in. It's not sexy, but it really makes a difference. Patrice?"

The girl at the front desk hopped up.

"Use the TGIN line for her—double wash, condition, hydrating mask, then plastic wrap and a bonnet under the dryer for twenty-five minutes. I'll take her from there."

As Patrice began washing my hair, I closed my eyes and let out a contented sigh. The warm water felt so good on my scalp. I could doze off right there in the chair if the salon wasn't so full of gossipy chatter.

"So, Eugene sat in on that breakfast meeting with KC and Clark Roland from the bank," said Angela from her chair next to Aunt Cara. "He thought it went really well. They want to do major renovations, and it's about time. Those branches look every bit of almost one hundred years old."

"That'll be good news if it means jobs," Tamera said. "Those companies Mayor Adams contracted were cutting corners, and they weren't hiring anybody local."

"Two strikes against them," added Leslie. "So, after that breakfast meeting, Kade met with Reid Gallagher—y'all remember him? Cliff's son? Looks just like him. Apparently, the talk of the town is how he was planning to come through and wreck shit, put people out of business and whatnot."

I willed myself to not react and was mentally thankful that my aunt was nosy. "I certainly hope Kade set him right?"

"He did. And so did I," Leslie said. "The meeting went well if I had to guess from the laughter and handshaking. If Sterling & Gallagher could pick up where Kade needs them to—"

"Eugene says it's a huge project. Reid doesn't live here, hasn't lived here since he graduated from Healy. He can't run it from wherever his business is headquartered."

"To your point, Angela," said Leslie. "Kade does want the work to be centered here. Potter Lake developer, Potter Lake workers. He wants Reid's company to set up an office here and work out of Potter Lake until the project is complete."

"Well, that seems like an easy solution," said Aunt Cara. "Reid seems to be enjoying his visit to Potter Lake. It wouldn't be the worst thing if he spent more time here. Near his parents, you know."

"And he's not bad looking, either," Leslie added, reading my mind. "He needs to be careful—one of these women around here will snatch him right up. Ms. Cara, you haven't seen any ladies over there trying to visit Reid, have you?"

My aunt laughed. I could tell she was doing her best to appear impartial. "I'm a busy old lady. I don't have the time to watch over there, but you know Patricia would not have that, anyway."

My hair had been washed, conditioner combed through, and rinsed. Next, Patrice put on a mask and wrapped my hair before directing me to the hair dryers. The heat and gentle hum lulled me into a state of relaxation but drowned out the rest of the conversation. I wasn't worried. What I didn't get from Aunt Cara later, I would get from Reid.

But my heart thumped in triple time at the possibility that Reid could be in Potter Lake for an extended visit. It made the looming decision of where I would lick my wounds and rebuild my life much easier.

"Sabrina, how are you liking our little town?" Evonne asked after she pulled me from the dryer. I settled in the chair at her station while she pressed the pump with her foot to bring me to her level.

"It's been…an *adventure* so far," I said, flashing a smile in the mirror. "I've been surprised at how I'm enjoying being in a smaller town. It's charming."

Evonne's hands skillfully worked, coating my hair with her specialty shea butter mix. "Charming is a good word for it. You're from Atlanta, right? I went to college there… sort of."

"Sort of?" My brow rose in curiosity.

Evonne chuckled. "It's a long story, but basically… country girl moves to the big city for college, isn't ready for it, meets a cute, older guy, thinks she's grown, finds out real fast that she isn't."

"Uh, oh. Where did you go? Spelman?"

"Mmhmm. The man I was seeing left me at an off campus party with some other girl and I went *off*. A few concerned party goers put me in a cab back to campus. I thought I was hot shit and tried to punch a security guard."

Evonne laughed as her fingers flew, twisting the damp strands together.

"Anyway, after the Dean of Students was done with me, I was suspended, and my parents decided I was not going back. Instead, I went to Healy School of Beauty and did my internship here at the Curl & Dye. I dreaded it, thinking I would have women walking out of here looking like Anita Baker all day, every day—"

"And she did, for a minute," Tamera interrupted. "Before she found her groove."

"Thankfully, Leslie and Tamera had an open seat, and let me experiment. I started playing around with hair and color and started my website. The rest is history. I met my fiancé here; we'll raise our kids here. We are the future of this town and we're happy to be that."

Her eyes met mine through the mirror, an understanding in the look she gave me, as if she saw beneath the surface.

"So you're here for an...extended visit?" asked Tamera, wearing a Curl & Dye apron and pulling a flat iron through Angela's hair. "Sounds like some drama. How long you planning on staying?"

"Weren't you listening when Ms. Cara told us?" said Evonne. "Her husband—"

"I didn't ask about *him*. I asked about Sabrina. So, *Sabrina*..." Tamera planted a hand on a hip and stared at me. "How long are you planning to be with us?"

I had no option but to answer, apparently. "Yes, I'm on leave from the bank where my husband and I work. I'm sure you're all well aware of that situation. I'll for sure be here through the new year. After that? Who knows? I've been thinking about resigning."

Even Aunt Cara's head popped up at that. Her brows furrowed as her lips pursed in response.

"Adrian doesn't appear to be leaving Aegis Financial. It would be awkward to stay, especially after he filed for divorce and cut me out of everything. He's petty, but he's basically paying me to leave. I'm not above taking the money for a chance to start over. I can get a job at a bank anywhere."

I looked over at Aunt Cara, who seemed to be nodding in agreement.

"Potter Lake is quiet and comfortable. This town extended a warm welcome to my aunt when she was grieving the love of her life. I'm hoping I'll get an extension of that while I start over."

"These people are nosy and much too close and will know all your business tomorrow," said Evonne, "but it's the place where I got to know me as a person."

"Take your time, honey. This is a new season," Aunt Cara chimed in. Leslie pulled off her cape and handed her a mirror to check the finished look. Her hair brushed her shoulders and was a shiny, bouncy sea of silver waves.

"What is a new season is these two-strand twists! My hair has *never* looked this good. Evonne, your fingers are magic!"

Each twist was carefully formed and defined, elegantly framing my face. The pattern was mesmerizing. As I turned my head from side to side, the twists swayed gracefully, accenting my features as they fell below my shoulders.

"I love when I can play in a new head. Your old shop did a great job—your hair is healthy. It holds moisture and a style well. This should last you a couple of weeks if you take good care of it."

I ran my fingers through my twists, catching Evonne's recommendations while still admiring myself in the mirror. It was so good to be back in a salon chair.

"Since you'll be in town for a while, come on back when you're ready for a retwist. I might be out on maternity leave, but don't sleep on Tamera. She keeps Leslie's locs looking nice."

"That's right, I can work magic—Ma'am!" Tamera shrieked, grasping my hands to gawk at them. "What's going on with these nails? Is this a cry for help?"

I glanced down and laughed, resisting the urge to curl them inward to hide the ragged cuticles and chipped color. "I've been distracted, okay? I suppose I should get myself all the way together today. Do you have time for me?"

"I'll *make* time," Tamera said. "Ms. Cara, how about you?"

"I never turn down a bit of pampering." She tucked her

magazine back into her bag and leaned forward. "That reminds me— did I hear right that Macy Raymond is pregnant?"

"Again?" Evonne's jaw dropped, then her eyes narrowed. "Are you sure, Ms. Cara? That last baby ain't even off the breast yet! Carl got to stay off her—they *just* got back together."

"Wait...who just got back together?" I asked. "And already had two babies?"

"Carl is a prominent attorney here in town. He and his wife, Macy had been together about ten years when they split up," Aunt Cara said. "She came crawling back soon after- probably because the new man was looking for some easy kitty, not a committed relationship."

"Mmhmm," Leslie hummed. "And for sure, Carl was stepping out too. But the only one anyone was talking about was Macy."

"So, they reconciled and Macy immediately got pregnant. Talk about a surprise!" Aunt Cara slapped her thigh for emphasis. "She thought she was on her way to menopause."

Evonne shook her head and clicked her tongue. "That baby can't be more than six months old. Just barely sitting up by hisself and she got another one on the way."

"Now, call me a hater if you want to," said Angela, "but I don't think they're good together. Their neighbors say they don't do much of nothin' but bicker and have sex."

"Carl's mama told me that she thinks Macy is still messing around behind his back," said Tamera. She fluffed Angela's hair, flipping it in front of her shoulders before muttering, "Ten dollars says that baby ain't Carl's."

"Oh?" Cara's brows hiked an extra inch. "You don't say? Meanwhile, she's leadin' Carl around by his man parts. He'll be retirement age with high schoolers."

I could hardly keep up with the gossip—my head swung back and forth, following the volley of conversation.

The front door to the salon swung open and a tall man with a large backpack strolled in. "Hey, y'all!" he shouted, arms open wide. "I got electronics, drinks, and snacks. Anybody hungry?"

"Right on time," said Leslie, hanging up her apron. "I need a snack to go with this tea. What you got in that bag that's chocolate, Zeke?"

Chapter Ten

Reid

THE AUDITORIUM at the recreation center was alive with chatter and laughter. Despite trying to push it aside, nostalgia washed over me as I realized that this room was where my father and his father and *his* father built the town of Potter Lake from scratch, where they had poured blood, sweat, and tears into creating a place to call home.

And now, after so many years away, I was back to do my part in keeping this town alive.

"Has it been weird to be home?" Sabrina asked, her eyes scanning the faces around us.

"Yes and no. It's been ages since I was here. I almost didn't recognize some of these people. The others..." I exhaled, shaking my head. "If anything, it shows me that time never stops. Some people that were approaching middle age when I left are kind of...feeble."

Sabrina leaned in closer, her warm breath tickling my ear. "Do you ever wonder what life would have been like if you had stayed?"

"Not once." I shook my head, then caught her eye. "I wouldn't be doing what I'm doing now if I hadn't left. We can't escape our roots, though."

Larry Cable, City Council President, called the meeting to order with a few bangs of a gavel, and the chatter died down. After the opening prayer and touching on several general topics, he moved on to new business and turned the microphone over to KC.

"I'd like to introduce Clark Roland, President of Potter Lake Bank," said KC, leaning over the podium at the head of the table. "He's been working closely with my office to discuss renovations to the bank's existing branches and plans to build a new structure on the east side of town. Clark?"

"Thank you, Mayor Cavanaugh," Clark began, adjusting his microphone.

He was a tall, thin man with a full head of dark hair, despite appearing to be the same age as my father. He spoke slowly with a deep tenor, exuding a quiet authority that demanded attention.

"As many of you are aware, Potter Lake Bank has been a vital part of our community for many years. It was the first bank in our town, and for a while, it was the only bank. As we grow, so does the need for services. We have been working with the mayor and city planners to not only update our branches but expand into the rapidly developing east side of town. This will provide convenience to residents in that area—"

"And jobs!" yelled someone in the crowd.

Clark acknowledged the comment with a nod. "In addition to improving the job market, our goal is for the next iteration of the bank to be done responsibly and sustainably. We will ensure that Potter Lake remains a beautiful and thriving community for generations to come."

"Absolutely, Mr. Roland," KC chimed in. "We've been

back and forth on this issue because I want the work to stay here in this community. That's where Reid Gallagher comes in. Reid, can you stand so we can all gawk at you?"

All heads turned toward me. I stood and awkwardly waved.

"Reid, as many of you know, was born and raised right here in Potter Lake. He's one of...well, *you*. He's built a successful career in land development, and we're fortunate to have him visiting his folks, Cliff and Patricia, who own Pinkney's Grocery."

I addressed the room, my eyes scanning the attentive faces. "Thank you for the invitation. It's an honor to be here, and I'm excited to explore opportunities. Let me assure everyone, including Patricia Gallagher, that I am not here to disrupt or shut down any businesses. The mayor has made it clear that he's looking for a partnership, and I'm in full agreement."

I sat back down and released a calming breath.

"The floor is open for questions," Larry announced. His eyes searched the room for raised hands.

A woman in the back row stood and waited for a microphone to be passed to her. "What is the timeline for renovations and the new branch? How long are we going to have piles of dirt and construction noise goin' on?"

"Great question," Clark responded. "We plan to begin renovations on our existing branches in the new year, likely breaking ground in the spring, depending on how quickly plans come together. The long-range goal would be completion within twelve months, but we'd like to have them operational before the end of the year."

He paused to shift his balance, clearing his throat. "As for the new branch, we're still in the early stages of planning, but we're hopeful that it'll be up and running within twenty-four to thirty-six months. Of course, our friends and neighbors will receive a construction schedule, so you will be aware of any disturbance."

"I suppose we can work with that, to get a bank on our side of town," the woman replied, nodding.

There was a brief silence before an older, bald and bearded man in faded blue coveralls and worn boots stood and motioned for the microphone. "Frank Crawford, Crawford and Sons. We were all here for the Quincy Adams fiasco that nearly tore this town apart, and I'm concerned about a repeat. We all know this is only the beginning—what is the mayor's office doing to prevent this growth from destroying what we've been trying to keep going?"

"I appreciate your question, Frank," KC acknowledged, speaking directly to him. "As the candidate that unseated Mr. Adams, my campaign promise was that every project would preserve the originality, the character, and the charm of this town. That's why we've been holding off for so long. I want a person in the lead that won't destroy us from the inside."

"I heard that," said Frank, and was echoed in the crowd.

"That said," KC continued, "I want to be transparent to the city council and with you all. Reid and I are in conversation about how we can move forward on this project together. His company, Sterling & Gallagher, would like to partner with us to bring change that will benefit everyone. Among other ideas is a mixed-use complex that would allow us to use the least amount of footprint for commercial and residential purposes—"

Larry raised two fingers, interrupting the mayor. "With respect, sir," he interjected, "the city has been hesitant to move forward with this project because you have stipulated that the developer and crew be local. Unfortunately, we are unable to fulfill that condition at this time."

"True," Mayor KC admitted, nodding at Larry. "So, my offer to Reid is contingent on his agreement to be based here, and that the crews doing the work are from this community whenever possible. Reid and I plan to meet again to discuss whether he can satisfy that contingency."

KC paused to laugh, adding to the low murmur of the crowd. "Zero pressure at all, Reid."

The room laughed, as did I, but the decision I needed to make gave me heartburn.

"Take the time," he said, nodding in my direction. "Consider the options. We wanted to make sure you heard the plan and the goal. Your agreement needs to be an enthusiastic yes before we move forward."

With a crack of the gavel, Larry Cable moved to table new developments on the project to a future meeting, then opened discussion on the next topic on the docket.

I nudged Sabrina and motioned her to follow me. We quietly left the auditorium, stepping outside the building. It was well after sunset, so the evening air was crisp, the night sky inky black and dotted with stars above us. I eased onto a bench next to Sabrina, the coolness of the wood seeping through my jeans. She sat close, her presence a comforting warmth against the chill of the night.

"I guess that went about as well as it could go without a definitive answer from me. Relocating to Potter Lake to run this project was not on my bingo card."

"It seemed like the mayor assumes you'll say yes," Sabrina said. "But I understand why you're hesitant. I know you feel pressured to accept this project, but you should sleep on it. Talk to some people, seek wise counsel."

I laughed and moved closer, draping an arm behind her on the bench. "Your counsel isn't wise enough? What do you think?"

"I think you're not ready to decide yet. I think you know that whatever you decide, I support it. So do your folks. So does…well, everyone."

"Yeah. Problem is, I think everyone would talk me into saying yes."

"Do you not want to? You can be real with me. I don't live here."

"Earlier today, I told KC that first instinct should be to run, to turn this down...but it's not. That...kind of scares me. But also?"

I landed a hand on her shoulder, walking my fingers to her neck. She shivered under my touch. I leaned in and captured her lips with mine. The kiss was electric, a surge of longing that had been pent up all day.

She shifted, moving closer, letting the kiss fade until our lips were no longer touching, but we were so close we nearly shared the same air.

"But also?" she prodded.

"But also..." I continued. "I felt a kind of *excitement* that I haven't felt in a while. I call it 'that new project feeling.' I keep saying I didn't come back here because the town is too small, there's nothing here for me. But these people that have come back here, that have made Potter Lake the center of their lives again...they seem happy. Life is simple and peaceful here. Maybe I've grown out of the life I thought I wanted to live when I left."

A chuckle bubbled up at a thought. "Or...maybe I'm mature enough for Potter Lake now."

Sabrina giggled. "Maturity sounds like your worst nightmare."

"One day I'll be blaming my aching knee on a thunderstorm comin'. My transformation to Oldhead or PopPop will be complete."

The sound of Sabrina's laughter at my worry of getting older both cut and soothed me. Weird how she was magical that way.

"I'll think on it. I know I'm delaying the inevitable.

There's a reason I'm drawn back to this place, but I want to be sure."

"If it helps," she offered softly, "I'm heavily considering our conversation about what happens after the holidays. I'm leaning toward not going back to the bank, which would mean extending my stay here. Indefinitely."

I reared back, trying to see her face in the faint glow of the streetlamp. "You serious?"

"Very," she confirmed. "I could spend months or years fighting Adrian. Or I could take the money and run. Stay here with my aunt in this little town. Maybe get a job at that bank they've been talking so much about. And spend some time getting to know you really, *really* well. That is, if you're staying."

She leaned in, lips pursed for another kiss. The sounds of cars passing by and the distant hum of conversation from the auditorium faded into the background as our lips met again. It was a slow, tender kiss filled with promise.

"That definitely sweetens the deal," I whispered as our lips parted.

"I thought it might. So, my aunt had a full day, and she's at home this evening. But... I saw your parents at the city council meeting." Her eyes rolled up to mine. "How long you think they'll stay out?"

"After city council, a bunch of them go over to the Kit Kat to drink and talk shit. I planned on taking you to dinner and debriefing the meeting, but..." I wiggled my brows. "You want to pivot?"

Sabrina's lips curled up into a smirk, her fingers tracing light circles on my thigh and gradually inching upward. "I think we need a change of plans," she whispered, her tone dripping with temptation. "We probably don't have much time. It's your house or a hotel room, and that would crank up the rumor mill."

I couldn't argue with that logic. I also didn't want to waste any more time talking when Sabrina could melt me if her fingers crawled any higher. "We could find a spot on the lake and hang out in the back of my SUV."

"Or we could have sex in a bed like adults and not risk getting arrested," she countered playfully and stood, pulling me up with her. "That would be even worse than the rumor mill."

I dropped an arm around her shoulder and tucked her in close. "Where is your sense of adventure?"

We walked through the nearly full lot toward my vehicle. I opened the door for her, and she hopped in. When she was secure in the seat, I closed her in, jogged around to the driver's side, and climbed in.

As soon as the car door shut behind me, Sabrina leaned across the console and melded her mouth to mine in a passionate kiss that left no room for misinterpretation. Her hands moved from my arms to my chest, eventually landing between my thighs where she gripped my hardening length and squeezed. I groaned into her mouth, barely able to contain the urgent need to be with her.

An appreciative, sexy moan curled from her as the kiss deepened. Our panting breaths turned the air inside the car so warm, the windows fogged over. I let out a low growl as Sabrina's grip tightened. I reciprocated by sliding my hand up the inside of her thigh.

Our lips reluctantly parted. I rested my forehead against hers, chest heaving. "You know how to stoke a fire," I rumbled.

Breathless, Sabrina chuckled, moving back and pulling the seat belt across her body. "You haven't seen anything yet."

I PULLED INTO THE DRIVEWAY, CAREFUL TO PARK FAR ENOUGH over that my parents could get into the garage when they came home. The house was dark except for the porch light that burned steadily from dusk to dawn. Sabrina followed me inside, her hands creeping up under my sweater. Her fingertips traced the lines of my muscles, sending goosebumps across my skin.

"You need anything? Water? We had some dinner left—"

Sabrina rushed me, leaping into my arms with so much force that she knocked us onto the couch. In seconds, we were a panting, groaning ball of limbs frantically pulling at clothes, the sounds of passionate and desperate kisses filling the air.

My lips roamed her body, exploring every curve and dip, tasting every inch. I was lost in the silk of her skin, the musk of her scent, the weight of her body pressed into mine. Her tongue licked trails of fire, igniting every nerve ending in their wake. Her moans filled the room, mingling with mine as we ground in rhythm.

The couch beneath us creaked and groaned under our weight, reminding me that we were in the living room.

"We gotta get up. Can't fuck on my mama's couch."

Sabrina's laugh grazed my neck. "Lead the way."

With a surge of energy, we untangled ourselves. I couldn't resist pulling her close, taking her lips again as we stumbled to the hallway, leaving a trail of discarded clothing behind us. I fumbled with the doorknob before finally pushing the door open.

The room was dimly lit, the glow from the moon outside filtering through the closed curtains and blinds. I tapped the light switch, bathing the room in the glow from both bedside lamps.

As soon as we crossed the threshold, Sabrina pushed me against the door and pressed her body into mine, working her lips down my body until she was on her knees.

"Baby, I don't think we have ti—*oh, shit.*"

I was deep inside her warm, slick mouth, my body already responding to her rhythm. My fingers curled into her hair while my hips tilted in a bid to get more of me inside her. She continued to take me deeper, her tongue swirling and teasing in all the right places until I couldn't take the wait a second longer.

With a growl, I pulled her up and walked us backward to my bed. The rest of our clothes were discarded, leaving us bare and exposed, skin against warm, supple skin. Her eager hand found me hard and pulsing, ready for the moment we were about to have. I caressed her body, teasing her clit until her hips rolled, seeking more friction, more heat, more contact.

"Fuck, I want to come! I need you. *Please*."

The desperation in her voice was kind of a turn-on. I grew harder as I stretched across the bed to the nightstand and pulled two iridescent blue foil packets from my toiletry bag. Tossing one to the bed, I ripped the other open. Sabrina watched intently as I rolled the condom on and gripped the base to ensure it was secure.

Our gazes locked as I leaned over her and wasted no time sliding into her, inch by inch until we were connected. I almost drooled, she was so warm, so wet. I had to concentrate to not come right away.

"Mmmmm...you good?"

"Fuck, yes...it's so good," she moaned, tossing her head back.

I began a slow, sinewy thrust, setting a steady pace that quickly escalated. We moved together in perfect synchrony, our bodies finding a natural push and pull. We indulged in deep, guttural moans and loud mutterings of pleasure as the room filled with intoxicating sounds. Our kisses grew urgent, breathless; our bodies became one being chasing ecstasy.

Sabrina's hands were everywhere, gripping my shoulders, trailing down my back, clutching my arms. Her walls clenched and pulsed around me with every thrust.

"You can go hard, Reid," she whispered, her breath tickling my ear. "Don't hold back, I can take it. Give it to me."

Sweat glistened on our skin as I eagerly complied, driving into her. We were both panting now, lost in the intensity. Every nerve in my body was on fire as we came closer to release. I reached between us and found her clit, rubbing it in tight circles as I continued to move inside her, intently watching her expression. I wanted her to come first, to watch her skin flush and her eyes glaze over before I let go.

"Shit, yeah, right there! Fuck, I'm so close."

Her hips bucked against mine in a frenzy. I shifted my weight, pulling one of her legs up to anchor against my chest, bringing her calf near enough to bite. A different angle meant I was plunging to new depths, hitting spots I wasn't hitting before. I continued to work on her clit, keeping rhythm with my strokes until her mouth dropped open in a long, throat-rending scream. Her pussy gripped me in violent spasms, her body writhing and convulsing beneath mine as she spiraled into orgasm.

Seeing her so sensual, so raw and vulnerable ramped me up, pushing me over. My hips shuddered against hers as I came in a chorus of loud moans.

We collapsed onto the bed, our sweaty bodies entangled, our breathing ragged as we came down.

"Fuck, I needed that," she gasped, still out of breath. "I don't think I ever knew that I needed that, but I needed that."

I laughed softly, brushing a tightly coiled twist away from her face. "Honestly? Me too. Been thinking about that since the last time we were together. And I've been thinking about how, if I decide to take that project…"

"And I decide to stay here indefinitely…"

"We're going to have to find a place where we can do a lot more of that," I finished, laughing.

"Uh, if you two are about done…" My eyes slammed shut at the creak of floor joists and the sound of my mother's voice. "I left your clothes outside the door here. I suppose you'll get them when you're...decent. But anyway, we're home, in case you figured on starting up again."

"Oh. My. God," Sabrina whispered, her eyes wide and fixed on mine.

"I don't even think He can help us," I said, sitting up and rolling off the bed.

I opened the door, grabbed up the pile of clothing, and ducked back in. She snatched up her bra from the floor and quickly put it on while I put on my jeans and a t-shirt.

"Stay here, alright? I'll talk to her, then come get you and walk you home."

"No! I'm not letting you face your folks alone." She stepped into her jeans, zipped them, and reached for her sweater. My mother had taken great time and care to fold it into a square.

"Sabrina, you don't know that woman. There's no telling what she's going to say."

"She'll say whatever she says to the both of us. You told me the other night that we were adults. I'm not hiding in here like a little girl. If you're going out there, so am I."

She bent to check her reflection, adjusted her hair, and pulled down her sweater.

I shook my head, watching her primp in the mirror. "You're a fearless somebody, you know that? I apologize in advance."

I grabbed her hand and led us to the living room where my parents were waiting.

"Hey, Mama. Dad. Wasn't expecting y'all home so soon."

"Seems like it," said Dad. He slowly rocked forward and back in his lounger, clutching an open bottle of beer in one fist.

"Y'all remember Sabrina, Ms. Cara's niece. She, uh... was—"

"We know what she was doing," Mama said. "Could practically hear it from outside the house. Glad nobody was walking by."

I wanted to laugh. I really did. But I didn't dare.

"Look, Mama… I don't know what you're looking for here. I'm not going to apologize for being a grown ass man doing what grown folks do."

"You don't have to do grown ass things in your parents' house, son. In your childhood bedroom." Her glare moved from me to Sabrina. "Lord knows your aunt won't have any problem with the two of you doing what you do in her house, but you don't have no business doing it in mine. I don't know how long you're going to be in town, little girl, but—"

"Mama!" I interrupted, standing in front of Sabrina. "Sabrina is a grown woman. She's not Elodie, so dial back the attitude. If you have smoke for anyone, have it for me."

"I got smoke for both of you because it was both of you in that room. Ain't no cause to bring up that woman you was married to just because I don't like this disrespect."

"Mama, I—"

"Mrs. Gallagher." Sabrina stepped around me, her hands clasped in front of her. "You're right. This was a poorly made decision on our part. I deeply apologize for the disrespect to your home. I'll grab my shoes and head over to Aunt Cara's. I hope you both have a great night."

The tension in the room was thick as Sabrina retrieved her boots and slipped her feet into them. I grabbed her jacket from the couch and held it so she could put it on.

"Goodnight, Mr. and Mrs. Gallagher."

"I figure you can call me Cliff," said Dad. "No need for formalities now."

Sabrina laughed. "Not a chance."

As Sabrina turned to leave, my mother turned her stony glare on me. "Well, you're walking her home, ain't you, Reid? Made her do all that hollerin', least you can do is walk the girl home."

"Yes, ma'am." I shuffled to my bedroom for a pair of shoes and returned to the living room.

The night air was frigid as Sabrina and I walked side by side down the sidewalk. One glance at her and I busted into the laughter I'd been holding out of respect for my parents.

"Oh my *fucking* God!" Sabrina wheezed, unable to walk a straight line she was laughing so hard.

"That meeting must have ended right after we left. I really didn't expect them to be back so early. I apologize for my Mama."

"Absolutely no need. But thank you for standing up for me."

I took her hand in mine, intertwining our fingers. "Would your ex have done that? Stood up for you?"

"Hell no. He'd have let his mother yell at me and told me to suck it up. *It's not a big deal, Sabrina.*" Anger flared at her words, though I knew it was an imitation of her soon-to-be ex-husband. I couldn't wait until she was free of him.

"I know the bar is in hell, but I'm at least trying to be better than him. You deserve someone who will fight for you."

We had reached the porch under the light at the front door. I pulled her to me and wrapped my arms around her, holding her close.

"Well…thanks for the night, anyway. I had a great time, even if we got interrupted."

"It was my pleasure. Truly."

"Some of it was mine. Especially all that *hollerin'*."

"Shit." My head rolled back, and I moaned, anticipating a long night. "She's going to fume tonight and bitch all morning."

"Should we give her something to bitch about?"

"We need to chill while we're ahead." I bent to kiss her, lingering in her warmth and how comfortable I was with her. "Can I see you tomorrow?" I asked when I pulled back.

"Whenever you like," she answered. "Send me a text. Or come over... My aunt is reportedly lenient about sex at her house."

I laughed, pulling open the screen door to turn the knob. As I figured it would be, the door was unlocked. Ms. Cara had a fire burning, and she was perched at the end of the couch with a pile of yarn in her lap. She leaned against the couch cushion with her mouth wide open.

At the sound of the screen door closing, her head snapped up. "Oh, goodness. I guess I took my sleeping pill a mite too early. How was the meeting?"

"We'll talk about it in the morning," said Sabrina, pulling her up from the couch. "Let's get you to bed before you wake up too much."

"Alright," she sighed. "Put the old lady to bed so you two can canoodle. Goodnight, Reid."

"I'm actually stepping out. My parents are expecting me back. I'll catch you tomorrow, Sabrina," I called, then turned the knob lock and pulled the door shut.

Dad was still in the living room, his eyes glazed over as he stared at the TV. "She went to bed," he said. "All clear for now." He chuckled as my shoulders dropped and I heaved a sigh of relief. "Bet that won't happen again, hm?"

"Absolutely not."

"We'll be laughing about it in a few years. Don't pay your mama no mind. You still her little boy. She'll be alright. But listen to an old man, son."

He kicked the footrest of his lounger down so he sat upright. "I know you're grown, but you got one divorce under your belt, and I'm goin' on fifty years married, so I might know a thing about relationships. A woman don't do all that hollerin' with a man she don't feel nothin' for, no matter what she tells you. Make sure you don't take advantage. Watch what she do, not what she say."

"I appreciate the wisdom. I'm listening. And watching."

He pushed himself up from the lounger with a grunt and slowly shuffled down the hall. I heard the door to their bedroom close, and only then did I exhale in relief. Once my dad was in the room, they were both in for the night.

Mama would have a fit if I did not change the bedding, so I stopped at the linen closet to grab a fresh set before I headed to my bedroom. Despite what my dad said, breakfast was probably going to be rough. I needed to get some sleep.

Chapter Eleven

Sabrina

Aunt Cara bustled around the kitchen, her soft voice humming in harmony with the sizzle of eggs cooking in a cast-iron skillet. The soft shuffle of her slippers sounded on the cold wood floors, adding to the comforting country ambience.

I wrapped one hand around a steaming mug of tea with honey and used the other hand to pull my thick robe closed. "Aunt Cara, are you sure I can't help? I can fry bacon. Or... make pancakes?"

"If I remember right, you're not known for your cooking skills." She laughed, glancing over her shoulder at me to make sure I was laughing too. "I've got everything under control. Most of it's already done. Relax, enjoy your tea. Finish telling me about last night."

"Oh, well..."

I got up from the table to stand at the counter and watch my aunt cook like I had for most of my life. She flipped the eggs with a spatula, careful not to break the yolks.

"Remember when your friend at the salon mentioned the

bank expansion? The guy that owns the bank presented his plan to the city council to renovate the two existing locations and build at least one new branch on the new side of town."

"It's about time," Aunt Cara said with a click of her tongue. "Those buildings are so old, I'm surprised they're still standing. They won't make it through the next summer storm."

She transferred the eggs onto a plate, then stepped to the refrigerator to pull out a package of bacon and a tub of butter. "Did they approve it?"

"Didn't even vote on it. Mayor Cavanaugh said he was talking to Reid about it. He wants the developer and the crew to be local, so nobody from Healy or Atlanta. Plus, he has ideas for other businesses to build on the land they picked out for the new bank location."

"Now that explains why the mayor asked to meet with Reid."

"Mmhmm. But Reid doesn't live here—"

"Yet," Aunt Cara interrupted.

"I think it makes sense for Sterling & Gallagher to have a satellite location here, but he can't make Reid move back to work on this project."

"Well, no. He can't force it, but given the history of this town, it is a fair stipulation. If Reid wants the work, he has to satisfy that requirement. Otherwise, we go another year or two with no development in town, and we sorely need new businesses, more housing, and better planning."

"It sounds like Reid is leaning heavily toward saying yes. At least for the short term. He has a whole life in Ohio."

"And a son in Atlanta. And…" She leaned against me, nudging me with her elbow. "A woman he seems to fancy in Potter Lake. You know how I believe in signs? Roland's wife is on my volunteer team. I can put in a word for you to pass along to her husband. Got to be lots of work you can do to build up a small community bank."

"Thanks, Aunt Cara. I'll consider it if I decide to stick around." I appreciated the gesture, knowing that having a connection could make all the difference in landing a job.

"If?" Aunt Cara raised an eyebrow, pausing before laying a strip of bacon in the pan. "Child, you change your mind more often than I change my socks. I thought you planned to stay for a while."

"It's an idea I've been kicking around, but nothing is set in stone."

"Something tells me your decision hinges on whether Reid decides to take this job."

"Not entirely. It would be a benefit, but I am starting to feel more at home here in Potter Lake." Aunt Cara smiled at my words, clearly pleased. "I want to keep all of my options open and not jump to this one because it seems easy."

"Maybe it seems easy because it's right. What does your attorney have to say about the divorce settlement?"

"Well, Gibson's firm is an offshoot of Kincaid Family Law. His mother is famous for slicing a rich man to the bone in a divorce. He's not as vicious as Sylvia, but he's not happy with Adrian's offer."

"The man is basically throwing money at you. What more does he want to ask for?"

"Alimony, assets, real estate." I sighed, taking a sip of my tea. "He believes I should at least keep one of the properties, if only to sell it for the proceeds. It would bring me closer to what I deserve. I don't want to fight Adrian…but I don't want to curl over and let him win, either."

Aunt Cara pushed out a grunt. "Before you know it, you'll have been trying to get divorced for years. The man has money and influence."

"And he's offering a lot of cash to walk away. I want it to be over."

"Your attorney knows best, I suppose, but—"

Before she could finish her sentence, a tapping noise

caught our attention. We looked up to see Reid standing at the back door, a large wicker basket in his arms.

"Well, how do, Reid!" Aunt Cara greeted him warmly as she swung the door open. A gust of frigid air rushed in. I shivered in my robe.

"Morning," Reid said, his voice a low rumble. He stepped inside, his breath visible in the chilly air. "Feels like it's never going to warm up around here."

Aunt Cara's face lit up when she peeked into the basket. It was filled to the brim with fresh vegetables. "Look at this gorgeous harvest! Cliff had a real good year."

"More than we can eat, that's for sure," said Reid, placing the heavy basket in the sink. "Mama wanted me to bring some over for you. She said to tell you to save her some soup stock."

"I sure will! I'm going to cook up some stock this weekend. I'll call her later to thank her. This is so generous—ooh, Sabrina! There's squash in here. I've got a taste for sautéed squash with roast chicken and wild rice."

My brows wiggled, and my stomach rumbled at the thought of a hearty meal. "Already looking forward to dinner, Aunt Cara."

Reid's gaze suddenly shifted toward me and he smiled, his shoulders visibly relaxing. "Good morning. You good?"

"Morning," I answered quietly. "I'm good. How...did your morning go?"

"My morning was alright," said Reid. "My folks have a busy day at the store, with the holidays approaching. I'll head over later to help them, but they left out real early."

"We were both lazy this morning," Aunt Cara said, going back to the stove to turn the bacon. "So we're just getting breakfast on. Hope you'll stay for a few bites. I made biscuits and sausage gravy, and we've got eggs and bacon for sides."

"I ate a little earlier," Reid said, "but I haven't had biscuits and gravy in years. I'd love a taste of that."

"Have a seat. Be up in a second."

Aunt Cara shooed me over to the kitchen table, where Reid had pulled out a chair and settled into it, then kicked out his legs. I grabbed a stoneware mug and poured some coffee for Reid, setting it down in front of him before sliding over the cream and sugar.

"Sabrina was just updating me on the city council meeting. I hope you'll make the decision that works best for you. Selfishly, we hope it means you'll stay. But while I have you both here," Aunt Cara said in a casual tone that didn't camouflage the curiosity lurking beneath. "You two seemed awfully tense when you came in last night. Did something...happen?"

Reid let out a deep groan and raked his hand over his face. I laughed at his dramatic reaction.

"Uh-oh." Aunt Cara turned down the heat under the bacon and came to stand at the table between Reid and I. "Too much silence after I asked a simple question."

"Um, well. We got caught acting grown last night." I suppressed a giggle at Reid's expression. "Patricia and Cliff walked in while we were busy and loud, so we didn't hear them."

"Let's be clear," said Reid, his pointer finger in the air. "*You* were loud."

"And *you* were busy!"

Aunt Cara's loud gusts of laughter filled the kitchen. The sight of her bent over and turning red was amusing, and the sound of her cackles was infectious. I burst into giggles again and, despite initial resistance, Reid laughed too.

"Oh, honey!" She gasped for breath between cackles and used a shaky hand to wipe tears of laughter from her eyes. "What did you think I meant when I told you to be careful?"

"I guess I learned my lesson. Patricia went hard on Reid, but in my defense, they were supposed to go to the Kit Kat for a drink and an hour of shit talking. We thought we had more time."

"You should have asked me—the Kit Kat was closed for a private event." She glanced at Reid, who, except for deep chuckles, had been quiet. "How are you holding up? I imagine breakfast was rough."

Reid shifted in his seat to face me, his mug of coffee aloft. "I remember all the times I snuck around when I lived here. It was bound to catch up to me eventually. My parents and I have a pretty good relationship because there are certain things we don't talk about."

He took a sip of his coffee, glancing down at the dark brew. "It's not about Sabrina. I knew better, but you know what they say about hindsight."

"I wasn't offended," I added, giving him a sympathetic look. "We didn't mean for them to find out that way, and we were definitely planning to clean up and hide it from them. At least it's out in the open."

"Don't know how good that is, but my folks are clear that I am an adult, I will date who I please, and while I will respect their home in the future, I won't be taking notes on who I choose to spend time with."

My heart bloomed in my chest. I hadn't asked for all of that...but would certainly have done the same for Reid if my aunt had objected.

Aunt Cara set a towel-lined basket of biscuits, a bowl of sausage gravy, and dishes of fried eggs and bacon on the table, then added plates and silverware before she took a seat.

"What's done is done, and all you can do now is move forward. Food's up, so let's dig in while it's hot, hmm?"

The clatter of plates and silverware, conversations and serving spoons was so heartwarming. I'd rarely experienced this in life, and I realized this was the kind of scene I craved. Between bites of fluffy biscuits and creamy sausage gravy, Reid and I exchanged playful glances across the table.

"I was thinking. You're always welcome here, Sabrina, but if you are staying on, you should look into a short-term rental in town. That way, you can have your own space, and you don't have to worry about...*imposing*."

"I don't know if I'm ready for—" My phone buzzed in the deep pocket of my robe. "Who the heck is calling me right now?" I mumbled, fumbling to grab the device.

My heart dropped into the pit of my belly as I pulled the phone out and flipped it over. The name displayed was one I hadn't expected to see anytime soon.

I STARED AT THE SCREEN, FEELING THE PHONE VIBRATE IN MY hand, flipping between the decision to let it roll to voicemail or answer his call.

Adrian and I hadn't spoken in weeks. It was his sudden, frequent off-site meetings, especially on Wednesdays, that made me suspicious. On more than one occasion, I followed him to the downtown Regency hotel and watched him walk out with an attractive woman by his side. She had a caramel complexion, a long, shiny, sable brown lace front, and thick false eyelashes. I'd stopped talking to Adrian after the second time I followed him to the hotel, but he was rarely home to speak to. I didn't think he even noticed my silence.

I excused myself from the table and walked into the living room before picking up the call.

"Yes," I said plainly, flopping onto the couch.

"*Yes*," Adrian mocked. "That's how you greet your husband? I haven't seen the whites of your eyes in weeks, Sabrina. Are you still at your aunt's house?"

"You had no problem finding me when you had me served with divorce papers. What do you want?"

The sound of his chuckle through the phone was arrogant and grating. "I want to know if you're okay, first," he said. "And second...I need to know what's up with the divorce settlement. It's been days. I expected you to have already signed it and moved on with your life. The offer is generous and allows you to walk away without drama."

"You couldn't care less about my well-being. And why would I need to walk away without drama? I'm not the one whose ass got beat on Instagram Live."

Adrian pushed out a bitter laugh. "When you have money and connections, you can make things like videos on the internet and men who oppose your dating choices disappear. Well, not disappear. If anything should happen to my attacker, I wouldn't want that to come back on me."

"Your *attacker*? The man married to the woman you've been fucking behind my back?"

"Uh, not too much on playing the victim, okay? I know you saw us together. Lauryn and that man aren't married. She made her choice. Short story even shorter, I need to know when your things can be removed from the condo. She's staying here, and I want to reduce the amount of stress that looking at your things has caused her."

My jaw nearly hit the floor. "Are you fucking *for real*, Adrian?"

"Jesus, Sabrina… Let's drop all of the faux surprise and ire. You were leaving. You think I didn't know that? Cut the shit and let's speed this along. We can stop pretending we're deeply in love and will miss each other. You'll miss my money and a penthouse apartment. I'll miss… Well, you were a warm body. And not a bad fuck."

"The surprise and ire isn't faux. I was blindsided by the filing and now…*wow*. You're literally replacing me with a younger model?"

"Man, I sound like a dick when you put it that way," he said, laughing. "I like to think of it as '*third time's the charm.*' So…the papers? And when can you have your things packed?"

"I don't know," I replied, swallowing the lump that threatened to choke me. "I need some time."

He scoffed, his impatience palpable even through the phone. "You've wasted all that time out there with your aunt that could have been used to find another place and move your things. It's not like I cut you off. You will not drag me through the courts, Sabrina. And you may as well know... Lauryn is pregnant. We want to be married as soon as possible."

"Oh. My. God." The man I thought I knew and had at one time deeply loved had transformed into swirling excrement in a toilet. "Who the fuck is this on my phone and what have you done with Adrian Ward? Specifically, the Adrian Ward who told me he had no interest in being a father?"

"Being real, I'm not overjoyed, but it will make Lauryn happy."

"Oh, *now* you're concerned with making a woman happy."

Though Adrian had an opulent corner office, shielded from most of the activity on the floor, I could tell by certain sounds in the background that he was at work. He played with a sand and rock zen garden to calm his nerves. The miniature rake made a scraping sound when he hit the side of the container. He also set a timer for his calls—every call. It began softly pinging when there were a few minutes left and it had been pinging every few seconds for the last minute.

I almost laughed aloud. He had only allotted ten minutes for this call.

"I can tell you're at work. So you're not leaving Aegis?"

"Hell no. I've got an open bid to join the board of directors. They said if I made the video go away that I'd still be in the running. It's gone, and everyone's back to work. You're the only one hiding out on a weak leave of absence, like people care about you and who you fuck. Look..."

I heard the distinctive squeak of his executive chair, then the thump of the chair hitting the credenza in front of the window. "Are you signing the papers, or do I have to call my attorney? I can make this painful and expensive, or I can be nice. I'll win either way."

His words lingered in the air like a dark cloud above me. Adrian had always been stubborn, but this callous, malicious approach was beyond anything I could have imagined.

"I haven't made any decisions yet," I told him, my voice steady despite the storm raging in my head. "I'm still in discussions with my attorney. Expect to hear a response from us soon. Don't call me again. All communications can be done through our attorneys, and I'll ask for everything I think I've earned and deserve."

There was a momentary pause on the line. "Don't fuck with me, Sabrina," he said, his tone dropping to a sinister glower. "You're not getting a penny more than I offered."

"You're the one with a pregnant mistress sleeping in the bed we shared, trying to rush this process. I didn't create this problem. You can wait longer than a few weeks while I get my shit together to make sure I get everything that is rightfully mine."

I ended the call, my heart pounding so loud I was sure everyone in the house could hear it. I tossed the phone to the couch next to me and dropped my head into my hands.

The weight of that conversation crushed everything inside me. Just as I began to spiral, someone sat next to me. I smelled Aunt Cara's perfume and collapsed into her arms, sobbing until I had no tears left.

"There, there," she soothed. "What did he say, honey?"

"He got her pregnant!" I wailed, sniffling as I sat up straight again.

Reid rounded the corner, worry etching his face and a folded paper towel in his hands. He handed it to me. I looked up at him, grateful for the offering but embarrassed that he was witnessing the death knell of my marriage. He sat in the chair near us, leaning forward with his elbows on his knees.

"She's pregnant. They're staying together—she's already

moved in. He's pressing me to pack my things and sign the papers so they can get married. And he's not leaving the bank. He called me weak for being on leave, and he said I was a...*warm body*."

"Sabrina, my dear, sweet niece," said Cara, her voice a soothing melody. "We're not shedding tears over him. Whatever you need to do to expunge him from your life, do that."

"I agree," Reid said. "He still thinks you're a woman he can control with money and a shit attitude about women. You're not, though. Right?"

"I mean..." I shrugged. "Not really."

"You're emotional because he blindsided you. Your feelings are hurt because someone you've been married to for a minute doesn't give a shit about you. But deep down, do you still love that dude? Do you want your marriage? Do you want to fight for it?"

I chuckled, my mood already lifting. "No, on all counts. I still don't want him to win."

"He lost *you*," Aunt Cara argued. "He has to pay you to get out of this marriage. You get funds to rebuild your life and live the way you want to live. Did he really win, Sabrina?"

I sucked in a deep breath and wiped away my tears with the rough paper towel. "So basically..." I sniffled, glancing from my aunt to Reid and back. "Y'all not gonna let me sulk and wallow in misery for even a *couple* of minutes?"

"*Aye*...sulk all you want," said Reid. "Divorce sucks. Grieve, process...but keep it moving. I've been through this. I know what has to happen in order to heal. But I also know you don't have to stop living your life to get there. I'm here for you."

"Like...*here*?" I asked, holding a hand out to him. He took it, an almost shy smile poking at the corners of his mouth. He *knew* something. "On the phone when you go back to Ohio here? Or...in Potter Lake for a long while here?"

Reid laughed. "I guess I can't keep a secret. I'm still working some things out with Mayor Cavanaugh. We've been texting since early this morning. He really wants to move forward, so he's giving me a little leeway. I'll be in Potter Lake for a minute, then heading back to Ohio to square things with Mitch. I'll be back and forth for a while, with long stints here in town. At least, that's the current plan."

I clutched his hand to my chest, curling it around mine and squeezing. "So, if I decide to stay in Potter Lake for a while...a *long* while..."

"I'll be here. In Potter Lake. I was hoping to take you back to Ohio with me, actually. Show you around, spend some time outside of this town. Really see how we get along."

The idea of a future with a man who already treated me better than my husband ever did made my heart flutter.

Aunt Cara clapped her hands and beamed at the two of us. "That sounds like a wonderful idea! I'll grab the paper to start looking for places to rent."

She hopped up, already on the hunt for her copy of the Potter Lake Times. "Are you wanting an apartment or a house, you think? Of course, you'll need furniture..." Her chatter faded as she disappeared into her bedroom.

I glanced at him, cupping his chin in the palm of my hand. "Reid, don't base a life decision on the possibility of—"

Reid cut me off with a kiss to my palm. "I'm not. I'm making the best choice for me and for this town, but like I said last night, you being here sweetens the pot. Now we have time."

He leaned in to kiss me but stopped before our lips could touch to add, "I look forward to getting to know you a lot better."

NOT THE END, THE BEGINNING...
***

Thank you so much for reading this steamy, festive ditty. I am planning an epilogue, but it will be a newsletter or supporter extra and will be released at a later date. I am excited to dip into the future with these two and see how they're faring.

If you enjoyed this novella, please take a few moments to rate and review it at Goodreads or the StoryGraph as well as your favorite retail site and your social media platforms. Word of mouth moves books!

Have a delightful holiday season, and I will see you in the next one!

WANT TO BE THE FIRST TO KNOW WHAT HAPPENS NEXT IN **Potter Lake? Join the newsletter— and get a free short story!**

Have you met my Potter Lake couples?

Potter Lake is a cozy mini-metropolis set in middle Georgia. After the collapse of the local economy, Potter Lake has shown resilience and a boom of growth, not only in residents but in steamy southern romance, beginning with the town's newly elected Mayor, former NBA star Kade Cavanaugh.

With KC's leadership, Potter Lake is set to become idyllic #relocationgoals and the place to be if you're looking for love.

Join Kade, Leslie and all of Potter Lake's funny, personable residents that'll make you wish they –and the town—were real.

- Leslie's Curl & Dye: Kade and Leslie
- Second Time Around (holiday short): Bennet & Sage
- The Guy Next Door: Taj & Evonne

Acknowledgments

I'm probably going to forget someone. As the old saying goes, charge it to my head and not my heart.

First to the fam I was born into, the fam I chose and chose me: *I love you all the most and then some.* Thank you so much for your support and enthusiasm for me and these books I write.

To my Wordmakers, the PDubs, the Trollops (Shaana, Terita, Anjel, Tanisha—you know what you did! LOL)—all my pockets of friends, you make life fun and worth living. Thanks for entertaining me.

YUGE thanks to **AdotK Edits**, who accepted my last minute pleading for her editing services and getting. me. together *with a quickness*. *You are a gift.*

Thanks to Christina at Paper or Pixels for this adorable cover. I saw it and I had to have it!

Books by DL White

Brunch at Ruby's, a Ruby's novel

Dinner at Sam's, a Ruby's novel

Beach Thing, a Black Diamond Romance

Elysium, a Black Diamond Vacation Romance

The Pearl at Black Diamond, a Black Diamond Romance

Leslie's Curl & Dye, a Potter Lake Small Town Romance

Second Time Around, a Potter Lake Holiday Short

The Guy Next Door, a Potter Lake Small Town Romance

Home for the Holidays, A Potter Lake Holiday Novella

The Kwanzaa Brunch, a Holiday Short

A Thin Line

The Never List

Hey, Lover, a Second Chance Romance

Unexpected, a holiday short

The Festival at Evergreen Falls

Grumpy Valentine

Calculated Risk *(Coming Spring 2025)*